The Insatiable Jane Travers

Isabelle Lauren

DEDICATION

To M who is my rock. A very, very sexy rock.

ACKNOWLEDGMENTS

This book would not have been possible without the help and support of a number of people.

Without the blogging community I would never have had the courage to write erotica. Thank you for pushing me and cheering me on.

Thank you to my beta readers, you know who you are. My book would not have been this good without your input.

Lara Zielinsky edited my novel and even though it sometimes hurt to hear some critical truths about my story, I'm grateful that she pushed me to make it better.

The beautiful cover is by CJ Douglass whose patience is unrivalled. She does amazing work.

And last, but not least, thank you, reader, for buying my book. I hope you like it.

.

CHAPTER 1

New York State, USA, 1926

"You're here!" Rachel flung herself in Jane's arms and kissed her.

Jane clung to her friend. Strictly speaking, Rachel had been her parents' friend, but after their death, Rachel had made sure to keep in touch through the occasional letter. Despite her being fifteen years older than Jane, Rachel had always treated her as an equal and Jane loved her for it. This was the first time she had seen Rachel in years though, as Uncle Henry didn't approve of her. Sadly, Uncle Henry didn't approve of much.

The drive upstate from New York City had been a harrowing hour in the two-seater; she had never taken it on such a long journey before. But she thanked her lucky stars that she had had the ingenuity to ask Charles, Uncle Henry and Aunt Lydia's driver, to instruct her in the art of driving. When Rachel sent her the invitation to come spend the summer at her country home, Jane had plotted to claim her independence, and driving lessons had been the first step.

Rachel pulled Jane into the entrance hall. Jane gaped.

The hall was big, with a high ceiling, and twin marble staircases leading down on either side. An ornate, crystal chandelier hung from the ceiling and Jane imagined how it would light up the room in sparkles at night. In one corner she spotted two armchairs with gold frames and scarlet upholstery, partly obscured by a large potted plant. The walls were covered in a lush gold and green paper, giving the space the illusion of a sun-lit plaza.

"Wow," she breathed. "Your house is amazing."

"Thanks to my father," Rachel said. "He gifted me a fortune in his will. But never mind that. How was your drive up?"

Jane exhaled. "A long drive like that is always a test of endurance. I feel quite ruffled." The drive up from the city had been stifling, but she was happy she had made the decision to flee New York City, right before the heat of the summer would make it unbearable. She took off her hat and gloves.

"You look ghastly." Rachel led Jane up a staircase. She turned around and shouted down the stairs, "Smithers, bring the bags to the Blue Room."

Jane didn't contradict Rachel. The journey had done nothing to enhance her already drab look. The wind had messed up her hair and despite the goggles and scarf her face was covered in dust and sweat.

In contrast, Rachel looked amazing. Her dress was made of a shimmery gold fabric and flowed over her curves down towards the floor. Despite the high neckline and long sleeves, the garment made Rachel look scandalously alluring. A headband encircled her short blond bob. Jane wished she could look as sophisticated as Rachel.

She smoothed down her own old fashioned gown. "I'm sorry. I'm in need of a bath, and Uncle Henry doesn't allow me to shop for myself." Uncle Henry forbade Jane a lot of things, which was why she had taken advantage of his and Aunt Lydia's annual summer trip to accept

Rachel's invitation. She was looking forward to a summer full of fun – Rachel had hinted at wild parties and lots of champagne.

Rachel waved away her apology. "I know, Henry was always a bore and I never knew why he was awarded custody of you. It's preposterous that you can't make any decisions with regards to your dress even though you are of age."

Jane shrugged. She agreed with Rachel, but there was nothing she could do. When her parents had died five years ago, Uncle Henry and Aunt Lydia had taken her in. She supposed she should be grateful – at least she hadn't been sent to work as a maid somewhere – but she wished her parents had made provisions for her once she came of age. Uncle Henry had prevented her being at the reading of the will and quite frankly, she was grateful for it. She would not have liked to hear how her parents gifted everything to Uncle Henry and Aunt Lydia.

"I've taken the liberty of buying some clothes for you," Rachel continued. "You'll find them in your room. If anything doesn't fit, I'll have Mary take it in, but I think you'll be all right. The dresses are quite forgiving. I'll get Daisy to come and do your hair; I reckon we can cut quite a lot off."

Jane had to rush to keep up with Rachel as she swept up the stairs and through the long corridors. The house was huge. She feared she could get lost in it. She hardly had time to process what Rachel had said about clothes and her hair.

Rachel stopped so suddenly, Jane almost walked into her. She opened a door. "Here you are."

Jane gasped upon entering the room. This was no mere room, but a suite. It was easily three times bigger than her room at home. The windows were floor-to-ceiling with French doors leading to a balcony overlooking the estate. There was a sitting-room and, beyond that, a bedroom with a large four-poster bed. Opposite the balcony Jane saw another set of doors. Rachel pulled her towards it. She threw open the doors to reveal a dressing room with racks of dresses. Jane had never seen that many gowns together outside of a dressmaker's shop. Between herself and Aunt Lydia they owned perhaps only a tenth of the number in this room.

"Do you like them?" Rachel asked.

Tears filled Jane's eyes as she nodded numbly. No one had ever done something this nice for her. She trailed her hands over the assortment of dresses, each more beautiful than the one before. She turned and hugged Rachel tightly.

"They're gorgeous, thank you so much." She wiped away her tears. "Are these really all for me?"

"Of course," Rachel said in a careless tone. "You deserve something nice and I have plenty of money. Besides, you want to look your best for Sidney." She winked.

Jane's stomach did a flip at the mention of the name. It had been four years since she had last seen Sidney Fitzroy, the man she had been sure to marry. Uncle Henry had squashed those dreams when he stopped her seeing Sidney before she had turned eighteen.

"You're too old to be socialising with men now," he had said. "You're coming of marriageable age and your Aunt and I will decide who you'll marry."

Jane had protested, but it had been futile. Uncle Henry was an unreasonable man who believed the women in his household should obey his every command. Her Aunt had been no help; she, too, believed that a woman should obey the head of the household.

One afternoon, Jane had been able to sneak out of the house to see Sidney. He was packing to go to university.

"Jane!" he had exclaimed. "What are you doing here?"

"I needed to see you." She hadn't cared about how desperate she sounded.

Sidney's face had clouded over. "You shouldn't be here."

"Please don't let Uncle Henry keep us apart," she had pleaded.

He had taken her into his arms and had kissed her forehead. "I'm going away to university. We can't stay together even if your uncle didn't interfere. It's for the best, Jane."

"Is that really what you believe?"

He had gently brushed a lock of her hair out of her face. "You are not even of age, Jane. And I need to concentrate on my studies. It's best we do as your uncle says."

His words had sounded reasonable, but his eyes held an infinite sadness.

"Uncle Henry is wrong," she had insisted.

He had kissed her cheek. "He may be, but he's your guardian. He may feel different in a couple of years. I won't give up on you, Jane."

He had pulled her into his arms once more and this time his lips had found hers for a brief second. She had desperately wanted to cling to him, but she didn't want to make a fool of herself.

"Jane?" Rachel's voice interrupted her thoughts.

Jane took a deep breath. Seeing Sidney again would be fine. They were both older now; and Uncle Henry had not found a suitable man for her to marry yet. There was still a chance for her and Sidney.

She looked again at all the clothes in the wardrobe, feeling suddenly overwhelmed. "I don't know what to say."

"Don't say anything. You've already thanked me, now go and enjoy the dresses. You're here to have fun." Rachel hugged her. "I'm so happy you're here."

"Me too," Jane said. "You're just amazing."

Rachel kissed her on the cheek. "This is going to be fun. I'm looking forward to introducing you to a wilder side of life."

Jane laughed. "I'm looking forward to the parties you

were talking about in your letter."

Rachel winked. "You will love them. Just be warned: they may be a bit more risqué than you're used to."

Jane felt a flutter of excitement in her stomach. "What do you mean by risqué?"

"There may be sex involved in some of the parties," Rachel said bluntly. "You won't need to get involved yourself, but you may see more than you're used to."

Jane felt an inconvenient colour creep up her cheeks. Sex? What exactly did Rachel mean? Jane wasn't used to seeing anything, so Rachel's advice wasn't particularly illuminating. She didn't want to betray her ignorance though.

"That's fine with me," she said in a careless tone.

Rachel narrowed her eyes. "Are you sure? I know you've had a sheltered life and I wouldn't want –"

Heat flooded Jane. "I'm sure. Uncle Henry may have been strict, but he hasn't been able to prevent me from finding out about sex. I'm not a complete fool."

The lie didn't sit well with her, but the truth was too embarrassing to admit.

Rachel nodded. "All right, but remember you come talk to me any time you need."

"I will." Jane swallowed. What had she got herself into?

Rachel hesitated for a moment as if she was going to say something else. She narrowed her eyes, then shook her head. "Okay. I better go check on my other guests."

Jane hugged her. "Thank you again so much, Rachel."

Rachel smiled. "I'll see you later."

She left the room and Jane sunk down on the bed, overwhelmed by Rachel's generosity.

A knock on the door announced Smithers, who placed her cases in the bedroom. When he had departed, Jane pushed her beaten down cases under the bed. She wouldn't need those clothes. They looked outdated and drab in comparison to the gorgeous ones Rachel had provided.

Slowly she walked past the racks and boxes of clothes. Rachel had even thought to include undergarments. Her cheeks burned as she held up a pair of lacy panties from a drawer. They were soft and feminine and...sexy. She did not consider herself a sexy person – Uncle Henry had seen to it that she would be chaste and prude – but holding this pair of panties in her hand she felt a frisson of excitement. Rachel had provided her a chance to reinvent herself, to shed her conservative skin and become the sophisticated woman she longed to be.

She giggled and stripped off her dress. Throwing it into the corner of the room, she vowed never to wear it again.

CHAPTER 2

Jane arrived downstairs for lunch later than she had wanted. Picking out a suitable dress had been difficult. Not because she had nothing to choose from, but rather because of the sheer amount of choices. She had settled for a short black dress in the end, with capped sleeves and a dropped waist. When she had looked in the mirror, she had hardly recognised herself. Daisy had cut her dark hair in a short bob. It was shorter than she ever remembered wearing it. It made her green eyes look startlingly big. Had they always been this size, or was she just wide-eyed with excitement? Her legs felt exposed in the short dress and she had to resist the urge to pull the hem of her dress down as she descended the stairs.

She had butterflies in her stomach when she crossed the hall towards the drawing room where cocktails would be served. Rachel hadn't mentioned whether Sidney would be present for lunch or not. She wasn't sure whether she was ready to see him yet. What if his feelings for her had changed over the years? He had promised he wouldn't give up on her, but she had not seem him, or heard from him, since they had said goodbye that fateful afternoon.

Jane never found out what Uncle Henry had said

exactly. She had held out hope that Sidney would come for her once she was of marriageable age, but the years passed and he had never even written her a letter. His continued absence should have been enough for her to lose her feelings for him, but she hadn't ever stopped thinking about him. She had always held out the hope that Sidney had been forced against his will to cut ties with her, but did that mean that he had moved on? Or had his feelings for her not diminished throughout the years?

She was immensely grateful to Rachel for her make-over. She couldn't imagine facing Sidney in her one of her out-of-date dresses.

Laughter flowed from the drawing room. Taking a deep breath, she pushed the door open. Rachel approached her as soon as she stepped across the threshold. "You look absolutely marvellous!"

She grabbed Jane by the arm and led her to a small gathering of people. Jane tried to see if Sidney was one of them, but all the men had their backs towards her. Rachel grabbed a glass of champagne from a nearby table and handed it to Jane. Jane had never had alcohol before, but she accepted the glass with a nod of thanks.

"Lunch will be fairly informal," Rachel said. "Most of the guests will arrive early evening for the meal and dancing."

"You're having a party tonight?" Jane asked. Her stomach dropped. She realised she had hoped to have a quiet evening catching up with Rachel.

"It's always a party at Rachel's," one of the men in the group said. He was tall with blond hair and clad in a grey afternoon suit that contrasted beautifully with his tanned skin. In his hand he held a cigarette. "Hi, I'm Matthew Montgomery."

"Nice to meet you, Mr Montgomery." Jane shook his hand. "I'm Jane Travers." She tried to concentrate on the young man before her rather than looking past him to see if Sidney was in the room.

"Please call me Matthew. We're on a first name basis here."

"Matthew, Lillian, and Sidney are my house guests for the summer," Rachel said. "We're quite close and I'm sure you will fit in."

Jane's heart leaped up when she heard Sidney's name. She was anxious to see him.

Another man came over and put his arm around Matthew. He kissed his cheek and Jane felt her face flush. She had heard of men who fancied other men, but had never met one.

The man turned to Jane and held out his hand. "I'm Richard."

Jane hoped her face wasn't as red as it felt and shook Richard's hand. "I'm Jane."

"I will leave you with Matthew and Richard, if you don't mind," Rachel said. "I need to check on lunch."

Jane flashed what she hoped was a confident smile. "Not at all."

She tried to see Sidney among the other people in the room, but failed to spot them. A moment later and there he finally was, by her side, smiling broadly and still as handsome as ever. She tried to quiet the butterflies in her stomach, but to no avail.

"I can't believe it's you, Jane." His voice poured over her and she instantly felt safe. He still looked as good as she remembered. His dark, wavy hair was longer but his blue eyes were warm and she felt she could drown in them. He leaned over and kissed her cheek, making her knees buckle. "You look tremendous. Time's been good to you."

Jane snorted despite herself, thinking of her joyless existence at Uncle Henry's. "Hardly, but thank you for the compliment. It's good to see you, Sidney. How have you been?" She tried to keep her voice casual and light, but couldn't avoid a nervous tremor.

"How did you convince your uncle to allow you to come here?" Sidney asked. "I thought he had you quite well locked up."

Jane laughed. "I didn't. They left for the summer and I snuck away."

"That's my girl," Sidney said approvingly. "I knew that old bastard couldn't keep you locked up forever."

Did you wait for me? Jane wanted to ask. Or are you with someone else now? She took a sip of champagne to gather her thoughts. The fizzy drink was pleasant and she took another sip. Yes, she could get used to this.

"I intend to have fun here," she said. "Much better to be here than in the city. Especially with this heat."

"Oh, Rachel's parties are the bee's knees!" Matthew gushed. "You'll have so much fun!"

"You do realise what types of parties Rachel holds here, right?" Sidney regarded her with a curious expression on his face.

"Of course," Jane lied. She felt a blush creep up her cheeks. She didn't want him to think she was a naive little girl. Apart from the fact that the parties were supposed to be wild – and apparently had some element of sex – she didn't really know much about them. But she wasn't about to admit that. "That's the whole reason I came here. You have to live a little, right?" She flashed him a smile with a confidence she didn't feel and took another sip of champagne.

Sidney raised his glass to her. "Here's to having lots of fun." He winked and Jane's heart lifted. He was still the same Sidney – fun, friendly and gorgeous. She fully intended to make up for the lost years, and hopefully by the end of her vacation she would not need to return to Uncle Henry.

"Jane, let me introduce you to Lillian." Rachel was back once again. When Jane turned, she could not contain a gasp of recognition: Lillian Smith, her favourite singer.

"So nice to meet you," Lillian said in her husky voice. She grabbed Jane's unresisting hand and pumped it enthusiastically. "I've heard so much about you. Only good things, of course," she added hastily.

Jane realised she was gawking and shook herself. "I'm such a fan of yours," she gushed. "I can't believe Rachel didn't tell me you'd be staying here."

"Oh, I try to be as low-key as possible." Lillian smiled and Jane felt giddy at the brilliance of her smile.

She had never seen Lillian perform live. She knew Lillian performed in clubs in the city, but Uncle Henry would never let her go to a club. And sneaking out in the evenings was impossible. So she listened to her on the radio as often as she could.

She had seen pictures of Lillian in magazines, but the pictures didn't do her justice. Lillian was easily a head taller than Jane. Her dark, curly hair tumbled down her shoulders and her eyes were brown, warm and smiling. She wore a silver sparkling dress, slightly longer than was the fashion and she stood with elegance and grace, her delicate fingers entwined around the stem of a wineglass. Jane was awestruck and realised immediately that she wanted to get to know this woman better. The others didn't seem in awe of Lillian, likely because they had already spent time with her. Jane drained her glass of champagne and racked her brain for something to say.

"So are you looking forward to the party?" Lillian asked. "Or are you not going to attend?"

"Of course she will attend," Sidney cut in. "Isn't that what she's here for?"

"I don't know," Lillian replied mildly. "Why don't we ask Jane?"

Sidney coloured and Jane bit back a smile. "Yes, I'm planning to attend," she told Lillian.

A woman appeared in the doorway and announced in a grave voice that lunch was served. Lillian threaded her arm through Jane's and led her to the exit.

Jane looked back to see Sidney out of earshot. "I have to confess I am not entirely sure what the party is about," she said in a low voice to Lillian. She felt Lillian wouldn't laugh at her ignorance. "Rachel mentioned something about sex." Even saying the word felt scandalous and Jane's skin pricked with heat.

"You'll love the party," Lillian said. "Stay with me and I'll look after you."

Jane exhaled with relief. Lillian had not laughed at her. Not only that: she was going to spend the party in the company of this gorgeous woman.

"I'm sure Jane will be fine," Sidney said.

Jane's head shot around, she had not noticed him coming up behind them. How much had he heard?

Lillian shot him a backwards glance. "Don't be jealous, pet," she said. "Jane's here for the whole summer, so you'll get your chance."

Jane let Lillian lead her to the dining room, feeling slightly overwhelmed. Her heart was lighter than it had been when she had come down for lunch. Sidney still seemed the same and if Lillian's tease was to be believed, he still held feelings for her as well. It was going to be a good summer.

After lunch, Lillian advised Jane to have a nap.

"The party will start late and you don't want to run out of energy just when things are getting good," she said. "I'll wake you up when it's time to get dressed."

Jane didn't need a lot of encouragement. The champagne before lunch had made her dizzy and that had only been one glass, albeit drunk quickly and on an empty stomach. A few hours later she woke, hot and disoriented. She had been dreaming of Lillian, although she couldn't recall the dream exactly. Her groin throbbed and when she gingerly slid her hand between her thighs she could feel wetness. This had happened to her before, but usually it was when she had been daydreaming of Sidney. She had never felt like this after thinking about another woman.

When Lillian knocked on the door a little later, Jane

was already up and dressed in a dressing gown.

"What are you going to wear?" Lillian asked without preamble.

Jane stared at her speechless. Lillian wore a dress that revealed more than it covered. The hem of her skirt barely covered the tops of her stockings. When Jane's eyes travelled upward she noticed that Lillian wasn't wearing a bra. A long necklace nestled between her breasts pressing the silk fabric against her erect nipples.

Jane pulled her thoughts back to Lillian's question. "I don't know. Rachel has lent me all these gowns and I haven't had time to find something suitable."

She led Lillian into the dressing room. Lillian started rifling through the dresses. She pulled out a red dress and held it up for Jane.

"What about this one?" she asked.

Jane frowned. "It's a bit short, isn't it?" She took the dress from Lillian and held it up in front of her. The skirt of the dress was fringed, which would leave most of Jane's legs bare.

"Not at all," Lillian said briskly. "You don't want to have a lot of dress getting in the way anyhow. Not if you want to participate." She turned and walked back to the bedroom. "Let's get you dressed."

Jane didn't want to show her ignorance, but she did want to know what she was getting into. Both Lillian and Sidney had alluded to the party being perhaps more than she could handle and she wanted to know why. She followed Lillian.

"Participate in what? Sex?" What did that even mean?

Lillian stopped and turned. "Oh dear," she said. "You really don't know what kind of parties Rachel throws, do you?"

She took Jane's hand and led her to the bed. They sat down, Lillian still holding Jane's hand. Jane felt apprehensive; Lillian looked so serious, she was worried what she was going to say.

"Are you still a virgin?" Lillian asked.

Jane's mouth fell open, but she couldn't speak.

"Well," Lillian prompted, a tad impatiently, "it's not a difficult question. Have you ever had sex before?"

Jane shook her head.

Lillian sighed. "I was worried about that. My advice: don't do anything tonight, just watch and learn. If you have any questions afterwards, I'll be happy to talk to you about it."

It slowly began to dawn on Jane what kind of party this was going to be. "It's a sex party, isn't it?" she asked. She had once read a story about this in a newspaper Uncle Henry had left in the lounge, although she could hardly believe they were real at the time.

Lillian frowned. "I wouldn't call it a sex party, it's a great party where people happen to have sex if they want to. But that's not the sole goal of the party. Everyone is just here to have fun, and for some people that means having sex. Don't worry, you don't even have to see anything if you don't want to, it all happens in the ground floor rooms, not the hall where the dancing is. But if I were you, I would sneak a peek anyhow. It's perfectly acceptable and you can pick up some handy pointers." She winked at Jane.

Jane felt herself grow hot at the thought of seeing others have sex. Aunt Lydia had briefly explained what sex was for and what happened during the act, but Jane had been too embarrassed to pay proper attention. The only thing she remembered was that it had to happen between a man and a woman and it was intended for having children.

She swallowed. "Will you participate?" She was annoyed at herself how shaky her voice sounded.

Lillian laughed. "I may, if I find the right person. It's great fun, though perhaps not recommended for your first time."

Jane wanted to protest that none of the people there were married, but she knew how naive that would sound.

She had left the world of Uncle Henry to search for a wilder life, and here it was. It was just a bit wilder than she had imagined.

Suddenly a nasty thought occurred to her. If this was what went on at Rachel's, then had Sidney also participated at these parties? Or worse: had Sidney slept with Rachel or Lillian? Her stomach clenched at the thought. That was not something she wanted to think about, much less witness.

"I'll leave you to get ready," Lillian said. "I'll meet you downstairs. Most of the guests will be arriving in half an hour, so I'll see you then."

Jane nodded, unable to speak. She was no longer as excited about the party as before.

CHAPTER 3

Jazz music floated up as Jane descended the stairs. She fought the impulse to pull the ridiculously high hem of her dress down. She had never felt so naked before, especially not in public.

The hall had been transformed beyond recognition. The ignited chandelier sparkled and illuminated the gathering of people beneath it. Jane paused on the stairs and took a deep breath. She was pleased to see that she wasn't the only woman wearing a daring dress. Most women were clad in similar fashion, but the range of colours was vast. Jane's gaze flew from woman to woman, taking in their bare shoulders and legs, the sparkling fabric of their dresses. She noticed a lot of women were wearing bejewelled head bands. She reminded herself to check her closet for head bands; Lillian and Rachel had worn them as well and they looked cute with their bobbed hair.

The men were not as versatile in their dress. In fact, they all looked similar in their tuxedos. The men Jane had met at Uncle Henry's had all worn tuxedo jackets with long tailcoats, but most of men here wore shorter jackets. Jane wondered if that was just a change in fashion or whether the men had taken the evening's expected activities into consideration.

The red chairs in the corner had been replaced, as was most of the furniture. A band was set up in the corner of the hall where Jane had seen the red chairs earlier in the day. She hadn't been sure she had wanted to go, but seeing the party assembled she was happy she had made the decision to attend.

Sidney made his way towards her over the dance floor. He met her halfway up the stairs and looked her up and down appraisingly. "You look fantastic."

She felt a flutter in her stomach. "You don't think it's too short?"

Sidney shook his head and the expression on his face was one of pure longing. Jane looked away, afraid her own desire might be equally evident.

They descended the stairs together and Sidney grabbed two glasses of champagne from a nearby tray which had been set on a tall table. He handed her one and she took it gratefully. She felt in need of all the courage she could get tonight.

"I'm just watching tonight," she told him, with what she hoped was a teasing tone of voice.

Sidney grinned. "So Lillian filled you in, did she? I was wondering when you would find out what these parties are really about."

Jane winced. She should have known he would see right through her bluff. "You or Rachel should have told me what the parties were about exactly. Rachel just alluded to it, saying there would be some sex. She didn't tell me it was a sex party! If Lillian hadn't filled me in…" She left the thought unsaid. A suspicion stole over her. "Did you just want to catch me off guard? Is that why you didn't call my bluff earlier today?"

"Maybe," Sidney said, still smiling. "But it's more fun now you know. Too bad you don't want to participate."

Jane's skin tingled at the thought of having sex with Sidney. While she would love that, she wasn't sure she wanted that to happen in front of a lot of other people. And Lillian had suggested she not participate on her first evening. Which seemed like sound advice to Jane.

"Are you going to have sex tonight?" she asked, trying to keep the wobble out of her voice.

Sidney shook his head. "No, I don't think so. I'll have too much fun watching."

A wave of relief swept over Jane and she smiled. She was about to say that they could watch together when Sidney spotted someone across the room. He excused himself and left Jane standing alone.

She took small sips of champagne while slowly making her way through the dancing people. She tried to find Rachel or Lillian, but saw no one she recognised. She didn't feel comfortable going to the various rooms by herself. While getting more educated about sex would be fun, she didn't want to be all alone in those rooms.

A hand grabbed her arm and she whirled around. It was Rachel and she looked amazing. Her dress was even shorter than Jane's and was cut low, so the tops of her breasts were showing. Jane found herself staring and quickly raised her eyes to Rachel's face. Rachel clearly didn't like to take half measures with her appearance. Jane felt a stab of admiration. If only she could live life as abundantly as her friend.

"Let's dance," Rachel shouted at her over the music.

Jane put down her empty glass and followed Rachel to the dance floor. She hadn't danced in years, but Rachel guided her through the complicated steps and it didn't seem to matter that she wasn't perfect.

She started to enjoy herself; the swish of the fringe of her skirt when she twirled around, the music throbbing in her veins and Rachel's hands on her hips elevated her mood from nervous to exhilarated. She received some appreciative looks and for the first time since arriving at Rachel's house, she felt free. She refused to remain naive and ignorant. She would learn; she was willing enough.

Sidney had said he wouldn't participate in the sexual activities, which made Jane feel hopeful.

The dance finished and Rachel led Jane to the relative quiet of the hallway leading off of the main hall. "I'm going to get Lillian," she said. "She mentioned she wants to join you in one of the rooms."

Before Jane could say anything, Rachel had departed. Jane took another glass of champagne from a passing waiter and leaned against the wall while she waited for Lillian. The music was not as loud here and Jane could hear sounds from a nearby room. Her curiosity piqued, she moved towards the half-open door. She glanced inside and felt her heart beat faster. The room was one of those Lillian had talked about. Some people were naked, sprawled out on the various sofas in the room. A few people stood around the edges, watching.

Jane could not see very well from the angle she was standing. Just as she was about to push the door open wider, she felt a hand on her shoulder. "Let's go in, shall we?" Lillian's voice said by her ear.

Jane looked back into Lillian's grinning face.

"This is what you are here for, isn't it?" Lillian teased. "What are you waiting for?"

She pushed past Jane, opened the door wider and swept inside. Jane followed her, making sure to close to door properly behind her. Lillian led them not to a spot along the wall, but an empty sofa with a great view of the room. Feeling very conspicuous, Jane sat down next to her. Lillian put her arm around her and pulled her into a more comfortable position. Jane stiffened.

"Relax," Lillian said, her voice husky and low. "We're just here to watch. Nothing's going to happen to you."

That was easy for Lillian to say, but Jane took a deep breath and berated herself for being so tense. Lillian was right; there was no reason to participate. She and Lillian weren't the only ones just watching.

Jane had never seen another adult naked before in her

life. Uncle Henry and Aunt Lydia had always covered up in her presence, not that she minded. But the people around the room seemed to have no shame in not only being naked, but being engaged in sexual activities as well. And it was not just men engaging with women. There were quite a few pairings that involved only women or a couple of women with a man.

Jane leaned back and decided to focus on the couple nearest to her. The woman was lying back in a deep armchair, her legs spread wide. The man knelt between her legs and was sliding his fingers up and down the woman's sacred place.

"Watch what he does with her cunt," Lillian whispered to Jane. "I can tell you that feels amazing."

Jane flushed. Cunt. She had lots to learn still. She felt silly for having called it 'sacred place' and was grateful she hadn't said that aloud.

The woman moaned and bucked her hips against the man's hand. Jane could see the woman's cunt on full display every time the man withdrew. Her whole sex shined with wetness. Jane watched in fascination.

The man started rubbing her more rigorously now, with great results. The woman moaned and writhed on the chair, occasionally crying out with pleasure.

"Do you want it?" the man asked, his voice low.

Jane felt herself respond to these words. She wanted this man to continue what he was doing. Her groin throbbed and she felt her panties getting wet. It would be a restless night tonight.

The woman nodded and said, "Give it to me."

The man needed no more encouragement. He raised himself up and Jane saw his cock for the first time. She blanched. Once she had sneaked a medical book off Uncle Henry's bookshelf and had looked at the drawings of a naked man. These had not prepared her for what she was seeing now. This man's cock was hard and much, much bigger than the pictures. She watched open-mouthed as the man took his cock in his hand and poised it at the entrance of the woman's cunt. He thrust his hips forward and his cock disappeared. The woman bucked her hips against him and moaned loudly.

"Such a tight cunt." The man moaned as he pulled his cock out and thrust it back in.

Jane felt her skin prickle as she looked at the couple having sex in front of her. Her own cunt throbbed almost painfully and she longed to slip her hand between her legs to relieve some of the pressure.

Lillian bent over to whisper in Jane's ear. "Let's get out of here."

Jane nodded. She had seen enough. Or rather, she would have loved to see more, watch more couples, but not if she couldn't get any relief herself. And she didn't want to expose herself in front of all those people. At least not   tonight.

CHAPTER 4

"What did you think?" Lillian asked Jane once they were back in the hallway. "Did you like watching that couple fuck?"

"It was interesting," Jane said carefully.

Lillian laughed. "Interesting? I saw how much you were squirming. It was quite hot, wasn't it?"

Jane didn't think she could feel any warmer, but her face flushed at the knowledge that Lillian had noticed her arousal. "Yes, it was hot." Why deny it? She sensed Lillian wouldn't judge her.

"Do you want to go back to the party?" Lillian asked. "Or..." Her voice trailed off.

Jane raised an eyebrow. "Or what?"

"Or we can have some fun of our own?"

Jane's heart pounded in her chest. It was not necessary to ask what Lillian meant by fun. "I...I don't know," she stammered.

Lillian regarded her. "Have you ever had an orgasm?" she asked. She didn't wait for Jane to answer. "I don't think you have. I can show you how to have one, if you want. If you'd rather go back to the party and dance for a bit and then go to bed, that is fine too. No hard feelings.

No judgement. But if you want to learn a bit more about what you just witnessed, then I'm happy to show you a thing or two."

Jane stood rooted on the spot. Her whole body screamed for her to say 'yes', but somewhere in her head she could hear Uncle Henry's disapproving voice. Only very depraved people focus on pleasure. She pushed the voice away, but some of her doubts lingered.

"I'm attracted to Sidney," she said, her voice shaky.

Lillian laughed. "That doesn't mean we can't have some fun. I'm only offering to educate you, I'm not proposing a relationship."

Jane considered this. Surely Sidney wasn't a virgin anymore. Wouldn't it be nice to show him that she knew a thing or two herself? She couldn't deny that she wanted a taste of the pleasure that woman had evidently been feeling.

She took a deep breath. "All right. I would like to know more."

Lillian smiled and took her hand. "Great. Let's go to my room," she said.

As Lillian pulled Jane up the stairs, Jane's mind raced. What had she got herself into? Would it hurt, whatever Lillian had in mind? Would she regret allowing Lillian to 'show her things'? But she pushed these thoughts away. Tonight she would enjoy herself. Become more knowledgeable about sex and have fun.

"Take your clothes off," Lillian said as she shut the door behind her. She pulled her own dress over her head and let it fall to the ground. "It's much easier and more fun if we're both naked."

Jane nodded. No sense being shy now, although her hands shook as she pulled her dress off. She followed Lillian's example and slipped out of her panties as well, pushing them underneath the dress.

Lillian took her hand and led her to the bed. "Why don't you lie down and get comfortable. I won't do anything you won't like and if you want to stop at any time, you only have to say."

Jane nodded and followed Lillian to the bed. Her legs shook and she took a deep breath before lying down. Lillian lay next to her and rested her hand on Jane's tummy.

"Have you ever touched yourself?" she asked gently.

Jane swallowed, her mouth suddenly dry. "A bit," she confessed.

"Show me," Lillian ordered. She sat up and moved to the foot of the bed.

Jane gaped at her. "I...I'm not very good," she said. "I'm not really sure I'm doing it right."

Lillian chuckled softly. "There's no one right way of doing it. Does it feel good when you do it?"

"Yes, but I'm always left wanting more."

"Lay back and relax," Lillian said. "Spread your legs."

Jane did as Lillian asked. She was naked, sprawled out in front of a woman she had only just met and she was more aroused than she had ever been. Was she a depraved hussy?

Lillian moved over her and kissed her softly on the lips. She trailed kisses down Jane's chin and neck all the way to her breasts. Jane sighed and started to relax. The kisses felt good and a low burn started in the pit of her belly.

"So perky and hard," Lillian whispered as she licked a path up Jane's breast. She reached the peak and sucked Jane's nipple into her mouth. Jane moaned as a wave of pleasure shot straight to her cunt. She felt her wetness dripping out of her as Lillian kissed, licked and sucked her nipple, tweaking the other one with her fingers.

"Feels good, doesn't it?" Lillian said hoarsely, looking up from what she was doing.

Jane could only nod, her breath coming in ragged gasps. She had never known she could feel this way. She had always viewed her breasts as just another part of her body, never realising her nipples could be so sensitive.

Her cunt felt as if it were on fire, screaming for some relief, but Lillian was not in a hurry. She lavished her attention on Jane's breasts until Jane felt she could no longer stand it.

"How does that make you feel?" Lillian asked, sitting back.

"Amazing," Jane breathed. "Like my whole body is on fire."

"Does it make you wet?"

An annoying heat rose up on Jane's cheeks, but she didn't look away from Lillian. "Very," she said, her voice hoarse.

Lillian grinned. "Isn't it delicious? Shall I continue?"

"Yes! No..."

"Yes or no?"

"I want more, but not my nipples."

Lillian arched an eyebrow. "Then what?"

Jane knew Lillian was playing with her, but she was past caring. "My...cunt." The word sounded coarse coming from her lips, but hearing herself say it made her bold, and even more aroused.

Lillian slid her hand down Jane's stomach and rested it lightly on her mound. "You want me to touch your cunt?"

"Yes," Jane groaned.

"Very well." Lillian let her hand slide down lower and Jane moaned as Lillian's fingers made contact with her dripping cunt. "Oh, so nice and wet," Lillian crooned. "You're a horny little girl, aren't you?"

Jane moaned, incapable of rational thought. She never would have thought hearing someone talk to her like that would make her feel so deliciously hot.

Lillian's fingers worked magic. Jane wasn't even aware of what she was doing, she just felt the waves of pleasure hitting her, the tension in her body rising to impossible heights. Lillian rubbed, pushed, slid her fingers through

Jane's slit, coating everything in her wetness. Wherever her fingers roamed, hot waves of pleasure shot through Jane. And just as she thought she couldn't take any more her climax hit her and she crested the last wave of pleasure, every fibre of her being filled with light. She cried out with delight as Lillian slowed down and lightly petted her sex.

"Oh my goodness," Jane breathed when she got her breath back. "That was amazing."

Lillian withdrew her hand and lightly kissed Jane's cheek. "That was fun," she said. "But did you learn anything?"

"I had an orgasm," Jane said. She felt wonderfully grown up.

"And how did you get an orgasm?" Lillian asked.

Jane frowned. She wanted to stay in this blissful moment forever, not be pestered by questions. "I don't care," she murmured. "It felt good."

"I'm glad it felt good." Lillian's tone turned stern. "But this was supposed to be an educational experience. So sit up, I'm going to show you a few things."

Jane grumbled, but complied. Lillian was right: she was here to learn a few things and she couldn't always go to Lillian if she needed some relief.

Lillian positioned her at the edge of the bed and put a stool in front of her. On the wall opposite was a large mirror and Jane stared at her own reflection. She had never viewed herself naked in the mirror and hardly recognised herself. She gazed at her small breasts with the erect nipples, at her flushed face and tousled hair. She looked like a hussy.

"Put your feet on the stool and spread your legs," Lillian said.

Much to her surprise, Jane felt herself getting aroused again. What was it about Lillian bossing her around that made her so wet? She did as Lillian asked and now she had a full view of her cunt in the mirror.

Lillian sat down behind her, her knees on either side of

Jane's outstretched thighs. Jane could feel Lillian's breasts pressed up against her back and the softness of her pubic hair against her butt. She wondered if Lillian was as excited as she was.

With one hand, Lillian reached between Jane's legs and spread her cunt lips open. Jane could see how wet she was. It was oddly mesmerising seeing her own cunt so on display.

Lillian pulled back the skin at the top of Jane's cunt and Jane saw a button of flesh spring forth from a hood of skin.

"This is your clitoris," Lillian said. She tapped it lightly with a finger and Jane gasped at the sensation this brought forth.

Lillian chuckled. "Yes, it's very sensitive. But it's not the only part of your cunt that can give you pleasure."

Jane watched Lillian's fingers play with her cunt. Now that the urgency for relief was gone, she could appreciate what Lillian was doing. She watched in fascination as Lillian's fingers slid lower. She gasped as Lillian slipped one finger inside her still-pulsing vagina. She leaned back against the other woman and she could feel Lillian's cunt wet against her backside. When it came, her orgasm was less intense than the one that had preceded it, but no less satisfying. Lillian hugged her from behind as Jane's breath slowed down.

"Now did you learn something?" she asked.

Jane giggled. "Loads."

Lillian moved away from her and stretched out on the bed. "I'm happy. That's what I wanted."

Jane lay down next to her. "What about you? Aren't you aroused?"

Lillian looked at her sideways. "Yes, I am. But I'll take care of it, don't worry."

Jane felt a stab of disappointment. She would have liked to play with Lillian's cunt, see it up close and try to make her moan as well. But she said nothing. Maybe another time she could convince Lillian to allow her to play. She was content for now. She felt as if she was cocooned in a cloud of bliss. Without shame or reservation Lillian spread her legs and slipped her hand between her thighs. Jane watched and listened as Lillian fingered herself to a hard orgasm, moaning with pleasure. Her own cunt started to throb with desire, but she was too tired to do anything about it. Then Lillian snuggled up to her and she drifted off to sleep.

CHAPTER 5

Jane was hiding. The garden was the perfect place for this. It was more like a park than a garden. The French doors in the living room opened up onto a patio from which a few steps led to a large lawn. To the left of the lawn a cluster of tall sycamores provided ample shade while to the right a path led through a rose garden. Jane had found a hammock strung between two trees set back in a secluded spot. From a nearby flower-bed the scent of gardenias was almost overwhelming. It was quiet in the garden with only the occasional song of a bird.

She had told herself that she just wanted to have a quiet spot to read her book, but the truth was that she didn't want to encounter anyone. Waking up next to Lillian, to the stark reality of what they had done the night before, had shaken her. She had quietly gathered her clothes, dressed as best she could and slunk back to her own room.

She didn't know whether any of the others knew – or suspected – about her and Lillian, but she needed some time to get her head around what had happened. To use Lillian's crude term from last night, she and Lillian had fucked. There was no denying it. And it had been amazing; she wouldn't deny that either. She had simply seen it as a lesson – a chance to know more about sex so that when she and Sidney were going to be intimate, she wouldn't be a complete novice. But somehow between last evening and this morning her feelings had changed.

Oh, she still wanted to have sex with Sidney. But she wanted to have sex with Lillian again as well. As she had bathed and dressed this morning, she couldn't stop thinking about Lillian. She wanted to play with her cunt and give her the same satisfaction Lillian had given her. Lillian's wetness against her back had aroused her and she wanted to trail her fingers through Lillian's cunt lips, find her clitoris and make her scream with pleasure.

Jane shifted in her hammock. Just thinking about Lillian made her wet again. But why? She knew she wasn't a lesbian: she was very attracted to Sidney and wanted him. So why did she get aroused thinking of Lillian? Sure, Lillian was gorgeous, with her swaying hips, long legs and smooth skin. But she was a woman. A woman with gorgeous breasts, which Jane wanted to kiss and fondle, making the nipples stand out like little peaks. She wanted to make Lillian moan and writhe with pleasure, crying out as she came.

Jane's hand crept down between her thighs and she pressed the wet fabric of her panties against her cunt. Her fingers found her clitoris under the thin material and she started rubbing. She closed her eyes, imagining Lillian in front of her – naked, begging to be taken. Jane's other hand fondled her breasts in turn, twisting and pulling her nipples until they hurt. She fucked herself furiously, using her knuckles to put more pressure on her clitoris. With a moan she came and she slowed down her movements, petting her swollen sex and caressing her abused nipples.

As she lay in disarray, Jane heard a voice call from afar, "Jane, where are you?"

Hastily she shot up and arranged her dress back over her knees and breasts. She smoothed her hair with her hands. Her panties were soaked and she suspected that the back of her dress hadn't survived either, but there was nothing to be done about that. Maybe she could quickly run upstairs to change.

She extricated herself from the hammock, but before she could slip away, the owner of the voice had found her.

"There you are," Rachel said. "Why are you hiding here?"

Jane forced a laugh. "I'm not hiding, I was just trying to find some quiet." She wasn't sure whether Rachel believed her or not, but Rachel didn't comment on it.

"We're going swimming. Are you coming?"

"Who is we?" Jane asked.

"Sidney, Lillian, Matthew and I. We'd love it if you came too. It's too hot to be out here anyhow."

Swimming did sound good and Rachel was right: it was very hot, even in the shade.

"I don't have any swim-wear though."

Rachel laughed. "You won't need it. Come on, it'll be fun. You do know how to swim, don't you?" she added as an afterthought.

"Of course," Jane said.

"Great. Then let's go."

Jane followed Rachel across the lawn and through the rose garden. They passed through a small cluster of trees onto another patch of lawn adjacent to a river. Jane marvelled at how large the garden was. At the edge of the water, Sidney, Matthew and Lillian were already waiting for them. To Jane's relief there was a small hut on the river bank from which Rachel took bundles of towels and blankets. She presumed Rachel would have swimming costumes in there for everyone.

Matthew and Sidney helped spread out the blankets. When all blankets were down, Rachel pulled her dress over her head. Feeling slightly self-conscious, Jane followed suit, slowly folding her dress and laying it on the edge of a blanket. When she straightened up she saw that Rachel was naked. The others were in varying stages of undress and

Jane hesitated. She wasn't used to being naked in front of people. Matthew and Sidney were down to their underwear and Jane's face flushed when she thought about the men being naked with them as well. Lillian and Rachel were now lying on the blanket, nude and seemingly unperturbed. Jane suddenly felt silly and naive; she had assumed that there would be swimming costumes in the hut.

"Come on, Jane, what are you waiting for?" Lillian said. "Don't be shy."

Jane glared at her, but bit her tongue. She didn't want everyone to think she was a prude. Quickly she unclasped her bra and let it fall to the ground. She stepped out of her panties and lay down on her stomach. She averted her eyes when Matthew and Sidney stripped their underwear off.

Rachel reached out and touched Jane's arm. "Are you all right? We're quite comfortable with each other, but if you'd like to go back to the house, I understand. I just thought that after last night you'd be fine with a swim."

Jane's skin prickled and she shot a glance at Lillian. Had she told Rachel what had happened the night before? She had thought that the events of that night would be private.

"I know you went in to watch everyone have sexual encounters," Rachel continued. "So I assumed you would be comfortable with a little nakedness among friends."

Jane almost laughed with relief. Lillian had not given her secret away. "I'm fine."

"Good."

Lillian winked at her and Jane felt her cheeks heat up. She watched as Lillian got up, her long legs gleaming in the sunlight. Jane's eyes fell on the patch of dark, curly hair between Lillian's legs and she felt a tug in her lower belly. She wanted to reach out, part Lillian's outer cunt lips to feel her wet core inside, the way Lillian had probed her the night before. Her nipples hardened and her cunt started to get wet. She pressed her hips into the ground, trying to stop herself from getting too aroused. It wouldn't do to show her arousal. That wasn't something she wanted to share with everyone.

"Who's coming in for a swim?" Lillian asked.

"Yes, it's too hot out here." Matthew got up too. Sidney followed suit and Jane, still lying on the ground, took a good look at him. He was as gorgeous naked as he was dressed. His muscles rippled underneath his skin and when she let her eyes wander lower, she had to suppress a gasp. His cock looked enormous, even though it wasn't hard. Jane had no experience with cocks at all, but after having had a peek around at the men in the room at the party, she could tell Sidney's was above average in size. But it hung soft and innocent between his legs, quite a different sight from the large, hard cocks she had seen the night before. Once again, her cunt gave a twitch. To have that cock thrust inside her while she clung to Sidney's broad, strong shoulders...

Jane sighed. Would that ever happen? Sidney had given no indication that he had any deep feelings for Jane, and she had no clue how to go about seducing him. If she got up to swim, he would be able to see her naked body and he would be able to make a decision right there and then as to whether he wanted her. There would be no slow teasing for her, no tantalising him with glimpses of her body underneath a dress. She would not be able to keep him in suspense as to what lurked beneath her revealing gowns.

She suddenly felt empty. This was not how she had imagined her courtship with Sidney when she had heard word that he was staying at Rachel's. She had imagined moonlit walks, long conversations, seductive dancing. Not this casual intimacy which felt banal. There was no seduction in walking around naked. She wanted to cover herself up, go back inside the house and wait for them all to return from their swim, but she knew the damage was already done. He had already seen her naked; nothing

34

remained to reveal any more.

"Are you coming, Jane?" Rachel called from the side of the water.

Jane was the only one still on the blankets. She had to make a decision, but she already knew she had lost. "Coming," she called and got up. There was no point in hiding her body, so she squared her shoulders, took a deep breath and walked towards her friends.

"So are you enjoying yourself?"

Jane turned lazily in the water. She had drifted away from her friends a bit, still feeling awkward about being naked. She envied the ease with which the others swam around. It likely came from them having done this before, but that didn't make her feel any less of an outsider.

Sidney swam towards her, a grin on his face. Her heart skipped a beat and she smiled back. "Yes, I am," she said. "It's different from what I'm used to."

"In a good way?" His eyes sparkled. "Or is it a bit overwhelming?"

Jane laughed. "A bit overwhelming," she confessed. "Uncle Henry and Aunt Lydia aren't exactly liberal-thinking people. I don't think I've ever been naked around anyone before."

"Except for last night," Sidney countered, swimming even closer.

Jane flushed. "What do you mean?"

Sidney was so close now that she could see the water drops in his hair, "I mean that I saw you and Lillian sneak off last night. I don't think you two had a cup of tea and a chat."

Jane felt caught out, but she didn't want to show her discomfort. She dove underwater and swam away from Sidney. When she resurfaced, he was next to her again. Despite the coolness of the water, she felt hot. She opened her legs to let the water cool the heat in her cunt. Thinking about what Lillian had done to her the previous night made her juices flow.

"What's it to you?" she asked, not ready yet to confess.

Sidney grinned. "Nothing," he said. "I just think it's great that Lillian takes such good care of you."

He swam closer, his hand brushing hers, sending sparks through her body. She wanted to wrap her arms around his shoulders and press her hungry cunt against his cock, but she stilled herself, floating as best she could.

"Lillian's great," she said. "I'm happy I met her."

"Yes, she is great," Sidney said and was it just her imagination, or did he put a lot of weight into that statement? She scrutinised his face, but Sidney merely grinned. "I hope she won't be the only one you'd like to play with."

Jane's body felt like it was on fire. She was surprised the water around her didn't evaporate into steam. She had no idea how to respond. Part of her wanted to scream, "No, of course not, I want to play with you too," and part of her wanted to flee. She did neither, but simply let herself drift a bit further away. Sidney swam to catch up.

"I'm sorry," he said. "That was very forward of me. Forget I mentioned it."

"No, it's fine," Jane said. The last thing she wanted was for Sidney to think she was not interested in him.

"I never forgot you, Jane." Sidney's tone was suddenly serious. "I hope you know that. I can't tell you how happy I was to see you yesterday and I want to spend as much time as possible with you."

Jane felt as if a heavy stone was lifted off her heart. She floated light as a feather on the water. She had longed to hear these words. Tears pricked her eyes and she looked away quickly. She didn't want to seem sentimental.

Sidney reached out and caressed her arm. Jane sighed. She wanted to melt into his body and allow him to do with her whatever he wanted. His hand moved higher, brushing her shoulder before making its way slowly towards her breast. Her heart pounded in her chest as she anticipated his fingers on her nipples.

Suddenly a cry disturbed the peace. "Get out of the water you two, the picnic's ready."

Jane's eyes snapped open, the atmosphere shattered. Her wet, swollen sex demanded more, but the moment was gone. She grunted in frustration.

"Can I see you tonight?" Sidney whispered as they swam back to shore. "I want to finish this."

There was no doubt in Jane's mind what he meant by "this". "Yes," she said. "Come to my room after dinner."

They waded ashore and joined the rest of the party.

CHAPTER 6

The swim left Jane tired and she retired to her room in the afternoon for some quiet time. She settled herself in the window seat with a book, but she stared at the pages without reading. She still felt aroused and the thought of having sex with Sidney both appealed to her and scared her. His cock was big, how would she ever be able to take him inside her? How did that even work? Lillian had put her fingers inside her cunt and that had already felt tight. How would she ever be able to stretch enough to accommodate a cock the size of Sidney's?

She flung her book aside with a frustrated grunt. Why had she agreed to see Sidney that night? They hadn't even courted yet and now she was willing to give her body to him? What would he think of her? She was making it too easy for him. After tonight, he would surely lose all respect for her. He'd see her as a plaything only, not the wife she wanted to be for him. And what if she fumbled? She had no idea what a man liked. Even the thought of having to handle his cock made her uneasy. What if she hurt him, or failed to please him?

There was only one thing for it. Jane left her room and knocked on Lillian's door. She hoped Lillian would be in her room; these discussions were better held in private.

To her relief, Lillian opened the door. "Jane," she said, surprise registering on her face. "Come in."

Jane stepped into the room she had spent such a lovely night in and the memories flooded back. She pushed them away. Now was not the time to be aroused. She needed her head cool.

"I was hoping you could help me with something," she said without preamble.

Lillian gestured to the sofa and they sat down. "Of course, what is it?"

Now that she sat here with Lillian, who was so much more experienced than her, Jane felt silly. She took a deep breath. "Sidney has asked if he could see me tonight."

Lillian cocked an eyebrow. "See you?"

Jane fidgeted with the fringe of her dress. "I think he wants to have sex."

"You think?" Lillian asked.

"I'm pretty sure."

Lillian smiled. "That's great, isn't it? Or don't you want to have sex with him?"

Jane wished her face would stop being so hot. "Yes, I do. It's just that..." She looked at Lillian.

"You don't know what to do?" Lillian guessed.

Jane nodded. "I feel like such a fool and I don't want to disappoint him."

Lillian laughed, her face lighting up with delight. "Why would you disappoint him? You're gorgeous and from what I could see of the two of you in the water today, he wants you as much as you want him."

"I'm scared," Jane confessed. "I don't know if his cock would fit. I mean, have you seen it?"

Lillian put her hand on Jane's thigh. "There is nothing to be scared of, I'm sure it will fit."

Jane grabbed Lillian's hand. "Can't you be there with me? Can't you show me how to do it? I don't think I want to do it alone."

To her relief, Lillian didn't laugh at her. She bit her lip and furrowed her brow. After a while she nodded. "I'll talk to Sidney," she said. "If he's all right with it, I'll be there for you."

"Thank you." Jane's heart suddenly felt a lot lighter. "I'd really appreciate that."

Jane twisted the fabric of her dress in her hands. She felt like a complete mess. She hadn't been able to eat much at dinner and had drank more than her fair share of wine. Right before dinner Lillian had whispered to her that Sidney had been fine with her proposal, but now that she was waiting for both of them to arrive, Jane had misgivings. What was she doing? It was one thing to receive a bit of education from Lillian as a friend, but this was much bigger. Was she really ready to give herself to Sidney? Would he not think less of her for agreeing to have sex with him so soon?

But the thought of not going through with it didn't appeal to Jane either. Just the thought of feeling Sidney's strong body on top of her made her quiver with anticipation. She wanted to explore his cock, feel his hardness. And if she was honest, she wanted him to touch her in the same way that Lillian had. She had dreamt of Sidney making love to her for so long, she didn't want to back out now.

A discreet knock on the door made her jump. This was it. She straightened her dress and smoothed her hair down. She took a deep breath and opened the door. To her surprise it was only Lillian.

"Come in." Jane pulled Lillian into the room. Lillian was only wearing her robe, the top opening slightly to reveal her naked breasts underneath. In her hand was a bag which Jane assumed held toiletries. Jane felt a tug of desire, but restrained herself.

"Where's Sidney?" she asked.

Lillian set the bag on the bedside table and sat down on the couch. She patted the space next to her. "He'll be along in a minute, I'm sure. We didn't exactly coordinate our arrival. That would've been a bit strange."

Jane sat down. "Sorry, you're right. I just thought you would both arrive at the same time."

Lillian put her hand on Jane's. "There is no need to be nervous, baby. If you want to back out, just say so. Sidney will totally understand."

Jane shook her head vehemently. "I am nervous, but I haven't changed my mind. I do want to have sex with Sidney."

Lillian leaned over and kissed her. Jane opened her mouth willingly to allow Lillian's tongue to slide in. She sighed when Lillian took her breast into one hand and caressed her nipple. Lillian's hands made her skin feel like it was on fire. She wanted more of her, but resisted the urge to let her desire take over.

"We're going to have a fantastic evening," Lillian whispered.

"Will you join in?" Jane asked. She didn't like the idea of Lillian being at the side line, watching them.

"Only if you're both comfortable with that," Lillian said. "I'll leave it up to you."

Jane reached out and slipped her hand inside Lillian's robe, fondling her breast. "I'd love for you to join in," she said. "I'll ask Sidney if it's okay."

Lillian sighed and briefly closed her eyes. "I love it when you do that. Let's just see how the evening unfolds. No need to orchestrate everything in advance."

A loud knock brought them to their senses and they pulled apart. Jane got up to open the door. Sidney quickly moved past her and closed the door behind him. He turned to Jane and took her into his arms. "I've wanted to do this for so long," he murmured as he lowered his head and fastened his lips on hers.

Jane melted into his body, her mouth willingly receiving

his tongue. He was so different from Lillian, who was soft and yielding. Sidney was strong, his skin rough against hers and his tongue demanding.

She gasped when he let her go. Her sex was soaked with her desire, her cunt aching for his touch. She felt silly that she had been so nervous the whole day; now that he was here, it felt natural to be intimate with him. She didn't object when he led her to the bed and helped her out of her dress. Clad only in panties, she lay down on the bed. Sidney stripped off his clothes and joined her. Jane panicked momentarily when she saw his cock: it was a lot bigger than it had been this morning by the river.

She looked over to where Lillian sat on the sofa and reached out for her. "Please join us."

Lillian smiled and let her robe fall to the floor. She lay down on Jane's other side and kissed her gently.

"You don't mind Lillian joining us?" Jane asked Sidney.

Sidney flashed a grin. "Of course not. I just want you to feel comfortable. And any man should be so lucky as to have two ladies willing to share his bed. Now let's get you naked too."

Jane lifted her hips as Sidney slipped her panties down her legs. He leaned over her and kissed her again, slowly making his way down to her breasts. Jane gasped when she felt his coarse tongue sliding over her nipple. Lillian copied Sidney's movements on her other breast and waves of pleasure shot directly to Jane's cunt, flooding her with desire. She wanted to feel the intense pleasure of an orgasm again, but she also wanted to explore Sidney's body first.

When Sidney made his way down to the apex of her thighs, she summoned all her willpower and gently pushed him away. He looked up, confused.

"Do you want me to stop?"

Jane almost laughed at the hurt look on his face. She struggled up into a sitting position. "I don't want to go too fast," she said.

"I promise I'm not going to hurt you," Sidney said.

"Maybe you can let her play with your cock for a bit," Lillian suggested and Jane shot her a grateful look. "You'll be her first and she should be comfortable with you."

Sidney looked chastised. "Of course. I didn't think. I got carried away because you're so gorgeous. We'll continue at your pace."

"Lay down and let us look at you," Lillian said, gently pushing him back on the bed.

Jane sat up and joined Lillian on Sidney's other side. Lillian took Jane's hand and lay it on Sidney's cock. It was big, hard and it pulsated slightly. Sidney groaned when Lillian moved Jane's hand from top to bottom.

"There's nothing scary about this, see?" Lillian said as she continued to move Jane's hand up and down.

Jane felt her cunt twitching and to her surprise she wanted to feel Sidney's cock inside her. "Will it hurt?" she asked Lillian.

"Not if you are properly warmed up," Lillian said. She looked over at Sidney. "Do you mind helping me warm her up?"

"I thought that's what I was doing," Sidney grumbled, but he winked at Jane.

"I have a few smaller dildos we can start with," Lillian said. "I can stretch her out a little before she takes you on."

Jane liked the sound of that.

Sidney grinned. "Let's do it."

"Lay down and spread your legs wide," Lillian commanded Jane.

Jane complied and Lillian reached over to the bedside table and grabbed the bag she had brought with her. She pulled out a few dildos. Jane had read about these, but had never seen one. Lillian held one up for her to see. "This one's smaller than Sidney, but will still stretch you nicely," she said. "We'll start with this and once you are used to its size, Sidney can fuck you."

Jane gasped at these coarse words, but not because they shocked her. She felt more aroused than ever, her juices seeping out of her into her butt crack. Sidney sat at the edge of the bed, his eyes on Jane's cunt. Jane felt exposed, and it made her feel wanton. She wanted Sidney to see how wet she was, how much she wanted him.

Lillian slid the dildo through Jane's slit, coating it in her juices. Jane bucked her hips, hoping to grind against the dildo, but Lillian poised it at her entrance instead. "This may sting a little, but let me know if it really hurts. I'll stimulate your clit as well to keep you nice and wet."

Jane's heart pounded. Lillian gently pushed the dildo into Jane's wet, hot entrance and at the same time she started strumming Jane's clit with her fingers. Hot pleasure shot through Jane and she moaned. This was such a different sensation; the dildo stretching her slowly, filling her cunt while Lillian's fingers kept sending sparks through her whole body.

"You're doing great," Lillian said, "it's almost all the way in."

Jane could feel the tension rising in her body, her whole being concentrated on what was happening to her cunt. The dildo slid in further and Jane marvelled at how deep it went.

"There," Lillian said with a last push. "All the way in."

"That looks so hot," Sidney groaned.

It had not hurt at all. In fact, it felt amazing. And even more so when Lillian started to move it in and out of Jane's cunt. Her vaginal walls clamped around the dildo and the sensation made her moan with pleasure. She felt close to the edge, that wonderful spot where she could let go, and crash on waves of ecstasy. But Lillian withdrew the dildo before she could reach that point. Jane grunted in frustration.

"I think you're ready for Sidney now," Lillian said. She bent down and kissed Jane's cunt, giving her clit a little lick. Jane's body spasmed.

"Sidney, take your place between Jane's legs. I'll take care of her clit. Just go slowly, but she is very wet, so it should be easy."

Sidney did as he was asked and moved between Jane's legs. He leaned over her and kissed her deeply. Then he took his cock and slid it over Jane's cunt, imitating the movements Lillian had made with the dildo. Lillian gently rubbed Jane's clit.

"Spread your legs a bit wider," she told Jane. "He needs all the room he can get."

Jane spread her legs as far as she could manage. She ached to be filled. Sidney positioned his cock at her entrance and started pushing. Jane gasped. The girth of his cock was significantly bigger than the dildo, and for a moment she thought he wouldn't be able to enter her.

"Relax," Lillian whispered, pushing her legs apart even more. "Don't worry, he will fit."

Jane breathed deeply and allowed her body to go as slack as possible. Sidney grunted as he slowly filled her hot, wet cunt. His cock stretched her wider than she thought possible.

"Just a little bit further," Lillian said, stroking her thighs and belly. "You're doing great."

Jane gasped. She thought he had already filled her up as much as she could take, but Sidney kept pushing, gently but firmly. With a last grunt he drove his cock deep inside her belly and she could feel it press against something at the top of her vagina. Pleasure shot through her and she bucked her hips against him.

Sidney bent over her and she looked into those lovely eyes. A deep sense of peace filled her almost as completely as Sidney's cock did. With Sidney fully inside of her, her heart soared at the knowledge that they were one. Tears pricked her eyes and she reached up and embraced Sidney, drawing him closer to her.

"Are you all right? Is this good?" Lillian asked.

Jane had almost forgotten she was there and she

reached out to include Lillian in her embrace. "Yes, it feels wonderful."

"Sidney is going to start now and I'll rub your clit. Is that all right?"

Start? Jane thought Sidney had already started. What was he planning to do? But she swallowed and said, "Yes, please rub me."

Lillian and Sidney laughed at her enthusiasm and Sidney started to pull out. The sensation of his cock dragging along the walls of her cunt was almost more than Jane could bear. Her cunt flooded with desire as his rock hard cock rubbed every inch of her vagina.

Jane moaned and she felt her cunt contract. Sidney repeated the movement and Jane lifted her hips to meet him, taking him deeper inside her. Lillian increased the speed and pressure of her fingers and Jane dug her nails into Sidney's back. She clung to him as he fucked her, his thrusts becoming more and more aggressive. She writhed and bucked underneath him, all the nerve endings in her body on fire. Soon she felt herself approaching that crest again, the edge of sanity where all the pleasure lay. She didn't think it could be possible to feel so much, her body light as a feather. And then her orgasm overtook her with a breath-taking intensity. She cried out as her cunt convulsed around Sidney's cock while she clung to him, feeling like she might drown in pleasure.

But Sidney didn't stop. He kept pumping into her and with the help of Lillian's expert fingers on her clit, Jane could feel herself approaching another climax. Sidney's thrusts became erratic and she could feel him stiffen even more inside her. Then a hot liquid filled her cunt and at the same time she cried out with her own orgasm, her legs suddenly weak and rubbery.

Sidney fell on top of her, his breath hot against her neck. Lillian lay next to them, raining kisses on Jane's face and neck.

Jane feebly pulled Lillian closer. She sought her mouth

hungrily and kissed her, her tongue seeking out the deepest places in Lillian's mouth. "Thank you so much for being here for me," she whispered when at last they pulled apart.

Sidney rolled off her and she whimpered when his now flaccid cock slipped out of her. "You were amazing," he said, still breathing hard.

Jane's heart soared at the compliment. She felt like Sidney had done all the work; she had just lain there and taken the pleasure he and Lillian doled out.

"I could definitely get used to this," she murmured as both Lillian and Sidney snuggled up beside her. She felt silly for having been nervous earlier. She turned to Lillian. "What about you? You haven't had any pleasure yet."

Lillian smiled. "Don't worry about me, at least not now. Why don't you sleep? You must be exhausted."

Jane smiled. She was indeed exhausted, but she didn't want to leave Lillian unsatisfied. Lillian smoothed Jane's hair and kissed her again. "We'll talk in the morning," she said and Jane felt her eyes close. Before she fell asleep she vowed to herself to satisfy Lillian in the morning.

CHAPTER 7

Jane couldn't keep a smile off her face the next day. She had woken sore, but satisfied, her whole body still buzzing from the pleasure she had received. Sidney had left the room in the night; his place in the bed was cold and empty when Jane woke up. Lillian had kissed her good morning before disappearing into the bathroom. Jane had wanted to explore Lillian and finally make her climax too, but when Lillian reappeared from the bathroom, she had been too nervous to broach the subject.

Jane hadn't seen Sidney all morning, and she was eager to find him and feel his strong arms around her again. After a fruitless search around the house, she gave up. Whether Sidney was avoiding her or had other business to attend to, she didn't know, but disappointment lay heavy on her chest. She started doubting the wisdom of her actions. What if Sidney had come to his senses and had realised that she was just a loose woman, ready to sleep with anyone? He must have known she had slept with Lillian, why else would Lillian have offered to guide her during their tryst?

She sought refuge in the library. Here she could calm down and think again. The happy glow she had woken up

48

with was wearing off. She saw herself through Uncle Henry's eyes: a sex-crazed woman, willing to sleep with anyone. Why would Sidney pursue her now that she had given herself to him so willingly? What remained to attract him to her? He had got what he wanted without even having to work for it and now he could easily discard her.

She could feel a blush creep up from her neck to the crown of her head. How could she have been so foolish? She didn't agree with Uncle Henry or Aunt Lydia on many things, but when it came to men, maybe they had been right. Giving herself up so easily had not been the right message to send.

Jane sighed. It had been such a perfect night: being pleasured by the two people she cared about most. She closed her eyes and could almost feel their hands on her body again, working together to give her more pleasure she had ever had. Sidney and Lillian had worshipped her and it had been so good. Surely something that good could not be bad? But how could Sidney view her as a potential wife after she had let him and Lillian defile her like that? He would be looking for a chaste wife, someone pure and innocent who would be a worthy mate for him. Not a lustful sex maniac.

Jane put her head in her hands. She had ruined it. By allowing her arousal to take over she had given up her chance of being with Sidney. She should have shown more restraint, not only with Sidney, but also with Lillian.

Lillian. Jane pressed her thighs together to stop her arousal from flooding her cunt, but she couldn't help herself. The image of Lillian, sprawled on her back on the bed, her wide open legs revealing her wet cunt was too much for Jane. Her own cunt throbbed with desire. She had wanted to crawl between Lillian's legs and explore her cunt with her tongue and fingers this morning, bringing her as much pleasure as Lillian had given her. But Lillian had woken up and broken the spell by announcing she needed to use the bathroom. When she got back, Jane's courage had deserted her and she had got up from the bed. The moment had gone, but now Jane regretted not acting on her impulse.

She shook her head. No, she didn't regret it, she had done the right thing. Seducing Lillian was definitely not the way to go. It had been one thing to be educated by Lillian, but now she was actually fantasising about pleasuring Lillian, licking those beautiful cunt lips, teasing Lillian's clit from its hood. And not only that, but she was once again wet with arousal. She could feel her panties becoming more than just damp. More than anything she wanted to put her hands between her thighs and finger herself to a climax. She knew she could do it, but she summoned all her willpower for restraint. She was going down the wrong path again. Thinking like this, allowing her arousal to dictate her actions, was a sure path to disaster. Lillian wasn't interested in her, and even if she was, Jane was not a lesbian. She could not have a relationship with Lillian. It was ludicrous to even entertain the idea.

And yet. Even if a relationship with Lillian was out of the question, why couldn't she have a little bit more fun with her? After all, it was summer and Jane had visited Rachel specifically to have fun and to let herself go a little. She had wanted to learn more about sex, and now she was in the middle of learning she was chickening out. And for what? Sidney needn't know that she wanted to have some fun with Lillian. She could still be wholesome and pure with Sidney. Maybe she could even tell him that she got carried away too much, that his charm was overwhelming. It would stroke his ego and take the blame off her for a bit.

Yes, that would be a good idea. Jane smiled. She could still rescue her reputation with Sidney. She didn't care much about what Lillian thought about her reputation. Lillian would likely be more appalled if Jane turned back to her innocent self all of a sudden. No, she could have fun with Lillian, enjoy more orgasms and get some much-needed relief. She laughed aloud. How much relief could she possibly need? She had just been fucked senseless the night before and again her cunt was crying out for more.

She shifted in her seat. Her panties were definitely sodden now, she would have to change them before lunch. They were getting quite uncomfortable. At the same time feeling her own juices soak the material made her even wetter. She spread her legs a bit farther apart and slid a hand between her thighs. She wanted to feel how wet she was, only for a moment. Sliding her fingers through her hot, wet slit made her moan with pleasure. She closed her eyes and imagined it was Lillian's cunt lips she parted with her fingers, Lillian's hot entrance she encountered.

She moaned softly as she slipped a finger inside herself. The fingers of her other hands circled her clit, teasing herself as she drew closer and closer to that little bud of pleasure. All pretence thrown aside, Jane began fucking herself with her fingers, all the while imagining Lillian on the receiving end of her hands. It was Lillian who bucked her hips against her hand, Lillian whose clit grew in size, Lillian who moaned her name over and over. And in the end it was Lillian's cunt spasming around Jane's fingers, convulsing almost painfully when the orgasm hit her.

Jane lay back, breathing hard. She lazily caressed her swollen sex as she waited for her heartbeat to calm down. She definitely needed new underwear now, and maybe also a new dress. Shame flooded her again when she came down from her orgasm high. Was she so sex-crazed that she couldn't even go half a day without sex?

She wiped her hand on her dress and straightened her clothing. She needed to change and she firmly resolved to ban all thoughts of sex from her mind. She crept out of the library, worried she might encounter someone who would ask inconvenient questions. She rushed up the stairs and into her bedroom where she stripped out of her ruined clothes and tossed them aside. If she kept this up, the wardrobe Rachel had provided wouldn't last her long.

Feeling deflated and slightly ashamed of herself, she redressed and went back downstairs.

CHAPTER 8

"Are you enjoying yourself?"

Jane turned to see Rachel next to her. She had gone into the garden, the house too hot to stay in. She smiled at Rachel, happy to have a chance to talk to her. No matter how hard to would be, she was determined to shed her feelings of shame and guilt. She had come here to have fun, not to mope around feeling sorry for herself.

"I haven't really had a chance to talk to you," Rachel continued. "Are you having fun?"

"I am having a lovely time," she said. "Thank you so much for letting me stay for the summer."

Rachel smiled. "Of course," she said. "I couldn't bear the thought of you being shut in with Henry and Lydia." She shuddered theatrically. "They're so incredibly stuffy, how did you survive all those years with them?"

"They're not that bad," Jane said. "I'm sure they mean well."

Rachel rolled her eyes. "If you mean that they want to turn you into a prude who never has fun, then fine."

Tears stung Jane's eyes and she quickly looked away. What was wrong with her? A few days ago she wanted nothing to do with Uncle Henry and Aunt Lydia and now she was getting emotional because Rachel expressed what Jane had been thinking all along.

"I'm sorry, I didn't mean to upset you." Rachel put a hand on Jane's arm. "I just want you to have a wonderful summer, that's all. And if you're having fun, I'm happy."

"No, I am sorry. You're right about Uncle Henry and Aunt Lydia and I don't know why I feel so emotional."

"Is it all a bit much? Being free all of a sudden can be frightening, but you're safe here. We all love you and my friends are your friends. We'd never hurt you, you know that, right?"

Jane nodded.

"And I know Lillian really likes you. She doesn't often take a shining to someone that quickly after meeting them. But if I'm not mistaken, you've already spent a night or two with her, haven't you?"

Jane felt a flicker of annoyance that her friend should know this. Were her movements monitored? What else did Rachel know?

"Lillian is lovely," she said. "She has kind of taken me under her wing."

"I'm glad. I don't want you to feel awkward or scared."

"I don't," Jane assured her. "It's just a bit overwhelming sometimes."

Rachel led Jane to a bench in the shade and pulled her down. "I'm sure that going from an oppressive environment with your aunt and uncle to the complete opposite in my house is a bit of a shock. But take your time. Getting in touch with your sexuality isn't always easy and it's very tempting to try everything."

Jane grew hot under Rachel's gaze. It was as if Rachel had read her mind.

"I'm not trying everything, but yes, it's definitely quite different. Not in a bad way; I just have to get used to it."

Rachel kissed Jane's cheek. "You will, it's only been a few days. There's no need to rush anything." She paused for a beat. "I'm having another party tonight. Are you up for it?"

Jane felt excited, but guilt followed immediately. Wasn't she supposed to put sex out of her mind? But then, she didn't want to miss the party either. She nodded. "Yes, I am."

"And maybe try to spend a bit of time with Sidney as well. He really likes you."

Jane blushed. "When did he tell you that?"

Rachel looked searchingly in Jane's face. "This morning, why?"

"No reason," Jane said, but her heart soared like a bird suddenly freed from its cage. Her behaviour the previous night had not repulsed him or changed his opinion of her. He still liked her, despite her holding no more secrets for him. Her feelings of guilt and shame left her. If Sidney didn't view her as a brazen hussy, then why should she feel guilty about loving sex?

A thought suddenly occurred to her. "Did Sidney tell you he wanted to spend more time with me?"

"He didn't have to. He said he likes you. You're not avoiding him, are you?"

Jane thought of the previous night and nearly burst out laughing. Avoiding Sidney was the opposite of what she was doing. But she wasn't ready to confide in Rachel yet. Not until she was sure that the depth of her feelings were reciprocated.

"No, I'm not avoiding him."

"Good. I'm not trying to play matchmaker here though, so please don't be pressured by me."

"I won't," said Jane. "I'm capable of making my own decisions."

"I know you are. You're still your parents' daughter, no matter how much your aunt and uncle have tried to change you."

Jane hugged Rachel. "I'm so grateful you let me stay here for the summer. Uncle Henry is such a bore and I don't know how much longer I could stay sane with them."

Rachel nodded. "No problem. But what are you going to do after the summer? Surely you don't want to go back to their house?"

Jane hadn't wanted to think about that yet. She had only been at Rachel's for a few days. She didn't want to ruin her time there. But the thought had crossed her mind. "I don't know what I'll do. I don't want to go back, of course not, but I don't see that I have a choice."

"Didn't your parents leave you any money?"

"If they have no one has told me about it."

"But they were rich, weren't they?"

Jane shrugged. She had never really thought about that. "I suppose so."

"What happened to your home?"

"I don't know."

Rachel frowned. "No one talked to you about your inheritance after your parents died?"

Jane shook her head. "No. I have to admit that wasn't high on my list of priorities back then. Besides, I was pretty much still a child."

"Of course," Rachel said quickly. "But you should have some idea of what happened to all that money. You can't live off your aunt and uncle's charity forever."

"I don't intend to," Jane said.

"You also can't just marry someone in order to get away from them."

Jane blushed. She hadn't consciously planned it that way, but she couldn't deny that when she had seen Sidney and all her old feelings had flooded back, the thought had crossed her mind. If she married Sidney, she wouldn't have to worry about where she could live any more.

Rachel grabbed her hand. "Jane, you need your own money. Without your own money, you are always going to be dependent on someone else. And if you're dependent on someone, you'll always have to adhere to their rules."

A flash of annoyance surged through Jane. "So if I

don't have my own money, I can't marry," she said. "That doesn't make any sense. Most women don't have their own money, so should most women just live with their relatives and not get married?"

"No, of course not," Rachel said. "I would just advise you to look into your inheritance. There must be something there."

"And what if there isn't? What if my parents had debts, or were broke? They didn't tell me about their financial affairs. Why would they? I was just a child."

"I doubt they were broke," Rachel said. "I knew your parents well enough to know they wouldn't allow themselves to get into debt. I bet your uncle is hiding something."

"Not exactly hiding if I've never asked him about it," Jane countered. "And to be honest, I have no idea how to ask him."

"We'll think of something," Rachel said. "I agree that it's not really something you can ask Henry about, from what I know about him. We'll have to use some subterfuge."

Jane sighed. She had visited Rachel get away from it all. To have a great summer of fun, not to be reminded of how unfortunate her situation was. But Rachel was right. She would be shackled to Uncle Henry forever unless she found out about her finances. She couldn't even marry without his permission. Besides, would Sidney really want to marry her if she was poor?

"We'll figure it out," Rachel said again. "I'm sorry I brought it up, I didn't mean to spoil your day."

"That's all right. You're right: I should be thinking of my future and not spend my time just having fun."

"At least have fun tonight," Rachel said. "Put it out of your mind and we'll think of something. The summer is still long."

"True," Jane agreed.

Rachel grinned. "Are you thinking of participating

tonight?"

"No!" Jane said, aghast at the idea. Or at least, that's what she thought her reaction should be. Her body flushed at the thought of having sex in front of people. The little voice in her head that represented her guilt told her to stay away from the party. She silenced it. Rachel was right: she was here to have fun, so she would. And maybe participating wasn't such a bad idea.

CHAPTER 9

Jane stood in front of the wardrobe, full of indecision. What did one wear to a sex party? She wanted to keep the option of participating open, but what could she wear that would say I'm willing to participate? She gave up and flopped onto the bed. Part of her was excited about the party, but part of her was terrified. It was one thing to fool around with Lillian and have sex with Sidney, someone she had known for years, but to actually participate in a casual encounter in a room full of people was a completely different ball game. Despite Rachel's caution Jane did want to experience it all. The thought of being back at Uncle Henry's without having tasted life at its fullest strengthened her resolve. She would not go back and regret not having tried everything.

Jane gazed at the open wardrobe and sighed. Although all the dresses were lovely, none of them were suitable for what she had in mind. With a frustrated groan, she let herself fall on the bed.

A knock sounded on the door. Jane lifted her head off the pillow and fought the urge to yell "go away".

"Jane, it's me, Lillian," Lillian called from behind the door. "Are you in there?"

"Come in," Jane called back and the door opened slowly.

Lillian entered the room and approached the bed. Jane rolled on her back and looked at her.

"You're not dressed yet," Lillian said, surprise registering on her face. "Are you not going?"

Jane groaned. "Yes, I'm going, but I can't find anything suitable to wear."

"What?" Lillian gestured to the wardrobe full of clothes. "There are so many lovely dresses here, how can you not find anything?"

Jane blushed, but maintained eye contact with Lillian. "I want to keep the option open of participation," she said. "But I don't know the best outfit for that."

Lillian didn't laugh at her, but merely nodded. Jane felt her skin prickle at the realisation that Lillian was treating her like an adult. Like it was not a huge deal that Jane wanted to engage in sexual activities with strangers.

Lillian walked towards the wardrobe. She was wearing a long silk dress like a kimono tied around her with a sash. "It's best to wear something you can easily slip in and out of if you want to participate," she said. "Like this, for example," she added, gesturing at her own garment.

She started rifling through Jane's dresses. She pulled out a pink silk one and held it up. "What about this one?"

Jane shook her head. "Too innocent," she said.

Lillian grinned. "Many people like an innocent girl."

"That may be, but I want to feel sexy, grown up. If I look like a little girl I'm going to be too self-conscious."

Lillian pursed her lips. "Come with me," she said. "I have an idea."

She pulled Jane along out of her room. Jane felt silly trailing after Lillian in her dressing gown, but they did not met anyone on their way to Lillian's room. Once inside, Lillian pulled Jane through to her bedroom and pushed her down on the bed. Lillian turned around and opened her wardrobe.

"You are about the same size as I," she said over her

shoulder as she rifled through her dresses. "I will lend you a dress." She turned around with a black silk kimono in her hand, similar to the one she was wearing. She handed it to Jane. "Try this."

Jane took it reverently. The silk was smooth and cool against her hands. She shrugged off her dressing gown and pulled on the kimono, but a cry from Lillian stopped her.

"What is it?" she asked, alarmed.

"You can't wear underwear with that," Lillian said.

"Oh."

Lillian smoothed Jane's hair away from her face. "If you do want to participate, you don't want to have to fuss with your underwear, do you? And if you took off your underwear, would you remember where you put it?"

Jane shook her head and she slipped out of her underwear. It felt natural to be naked in Lillian's presence. She pulled the kimono on, the silk cool and enticing against her hot skin. Lillian helped her tie the sash around her waist, then stepped back. She looked Jane up and down appraisingly.

"You look fantastic," she said. She pulled Jane towards the mirror. "Look."

Jane looked in the mirror and her eyes widened. The silk of the kimono flowed over her skin like water and it was abundantly clear that she was not wearing anything underneath. She looked sophisticated and grown up, exactly what she didn't feel, but wanted to be. She grinned and hugged Lillian.

"It's gorgeous, thank you so much," she said.

"It's only gorgeous because you made it so," Lillian countered. "Shall we go?"

They descended the stairs together. Despite Lillian's reassuring words, Jane still felt slightly apprehensive. The other party had been fun precisely because Jane hadn't known what to expect. But tonight she wanted to participate and now the stakes felt much higher.

Lillian grabbed two glasses of champagne from a nearby table and handed Jane one.

"Here's to a lot of fun," she said.

Jane toasted to that and took a large sip of champagne. The bubbles tickled her nose, but she could feel the alcohol coursing through her veins. Another large sip and she started to calm down.

She spotted Matthew and Sidney at the other end of the room. Lillian followed her gaze. "Let's join them," she suggested.

"Ladies," Sidney said with a short bow when they reached him and Matthew. "You look gorgeous, Jane."

His eyes lingered on her appraisingly and Jane felt butterflies in her stomach.

"Where is the band?" Jane asked, looking around. A gramophone player was set up in the corner of the hall, playing music at a quiet level. No one was dancing either.

"The theme is a bit different tonight," Matthew said.

Jane took a sip of champagne to hide her confusion.

"Tonight is a bit more...focused," Sidney explained.

"Focused how?" Jane asked, her eyes roaming over the guests of which there weren't that many.

"Tonight we drop any pretense," Lillian said. "It's a real sex party."

While Jane had fully expected to either participate in sexual activities or watch as much as she could, she still blanched. She had assumed it would be a regular party with some sexual side activities, not a party focused on sex.

"I'm sorry," Lillian said. "I thought you knew when you..." She gestured at Jane's outfit.

"It's fine," Jane said quickly. It didn't matter now, did it? She had planned to participate, so why did it matter that the focus was on sex tonight? Either way, she could have her fun. And yet, it felt different. If it was a real sex party, it meant that everyone would be participating. And that meant that all the guests could see her, too.

"Not everyone will be participating," Matthew said as if

reading her mind. "There's no pressure."

"You don't have to stay," Sidney offered. "We can go upstairs, have some time together."

Jane was tempted. She assumed that Sidney didn't mean they would talk and the idea of a night alone with him sounded good. But she remembered her resolve and shook her head. "No, I'd like to stay. It'll be interesting."

Sidney's gaze darkened momentarily before he smiled brightly. "Great, I'm sure we'll all have a lovely time."

"Will you participate?" Jane asked Matthew. It felt easier talking to him about it. Was that because she didn't lust after Matthew?

Matthew shrugged. "I haven't decided yet."

Jane looked around to see if she could see Richard, the man who had kissed Matthew on the day she had arrived. "Is Richard not here?"

Sidney laughed and clapped Matthew on the shoulder. "Matthew isn't picky whom he fucks. He doesn't need Richard."

Matthew laughed, but it wasn't a happy sound. Jane had the impression he didn't find Sidney's joke funny.

"I'm not really in the mood," Matthew said. "We'll see how the night goes."

Jane lay her hand on his arm. "I hope you have fun anyhow."

A warm smile flashed over Matthew's face. He winked. "I hope you do too."

Lillian took Jane's hand. "Let's get more champagne."

They waved a quick farewell to the men and made their way to the bar which was set up on the other side of the hall. "Are you sure about staying?"

"Yes, I'm sure." Jane put as much conviction into her voice as she could.

"The invitation from Sidney is tempting though. You'd still get sated but it would be less intense…"

Jane shook her head. "Maybe, but I vowed I'd enjoy myself and experience life. I'm not going to chicken out now."

Lillian grinned and kissed Jane. Their tongues intertwined and Jane pressed herself closer to Lillian. She didn't care who saw or what people would think, she wanted, no: needed, to feel Lillian's body against hers. At long last they pulled apart and Jane smiled. "I am definitely staying tonight."

CHAPTER 10

Jane and Lillian walked around for a bit until Rachel appeared in the hall. She clapped her hands to get everyone's attention.

"Ladies and gentlemen, you all know the drill. The rooms are now open for your enjoyment. Same rules apply as always, if you're unsure, please talk to me."

Jane decided to make a quick dash to the loo before joining the others in one of the room. The champagne had made her mellow and she was looking forward to the evening.

She entered the drawing room after her comfort break and looked around. The room was lit by candlelight and it was darker than it had been in the hall. She let her eyes adjust and took a seat on the sofa nearest to her. She tried to spot Lillian, but couldn't see her.

There were a number of people already in the room, none of whom paid attention to her. She could see why: they were all engaged in some sort of sexual conduct. Jane didn't know how to conduct herself. Should she sit back and allow herself to be aroused before joining in? And how did one join in?

It wasn't too dark to make out what was going on and

as Jane tried hard to look anywhere but at the people spread out on the various sofas and settees, she noticed others who just sat and watched. She was not the only person who didn't engage and after a while her nerves steadied themselves. Lillian and Rachel had both told her that she didn't need to participate; she had not realised that there were more who felt the same. Some people evidently only came to watch.

This realisation made her feel better and she sank back into the cushions of the sofa. It would be fun to watch and maybe she could pick up some pointers. She smiled to herself; leave it to her to make this into an educational session.

Her eyes were drawn to a group of people in the middle of the room. At the centre of the group, reclining on a lounge chair, was a blonde woman. She was completely naked, her legs spread wide with her sex on full display. She was close enough for Jane to see she was very wet. Another woman was rubbing her breasts, pinching her nipples. A man stood by her head and he thrust his cock in her mouth. Jane's eyes widened when the blonde took him completely into her mouth. How was that even possible?

Another man knelt between the blonde woman's legs and rubbed her cunt with his fingers. She wasn't able to speak due to the cock in her mouth, but she uttered a low moan. The man pushed her legs back so her knees hit her chest and he took his cock in his hand. He slowly pushed himself inside her and Jane moved slightly to get a better view. The blonde woman had two cocks in her now: one in her mouth and one in her cunt. She seemed to really enjoy it. The other woman kept fondling her breasts, every now and then reaching over to rub the blonde woman's clit.

Jane could feel her wetness gather in her own cunt. It looked delicious to be used and pleased by so many people. She shifted on the couch in an attempt to relief the throbbing in her cunt, but to no avail.

"She makes a beautiful display, doesn't she?" a voice said.

Jane looked up to see a woman standing in front of her, looking down on her. She was naked, but didn't show any sign of being self-conscious about this fact. She sat down next to Jane and held out her hand.

"I'm Laura," she said.

Jane shook her hand. "I'm Jane."

"Is this your first time?"

"One of my firsts," Jane confessed. "Is it that obvious?"

Laura shook her head. "No, I've just never seen you here before. It's great, isn't it?"

Jane looked at the blonde woman and her attendees and she gasped when the first man pulled his cock out of the woman's mouth and sprayed a milky white liquid all over her face.

Laura laughed softly next to her. "You're very new to this, aren't you?"

Jane turned back to her. "Yes I am," she admitted. "It's arousing though."

"Yes, it is. Are you just watching, or...?" She left the rest of the sentence hang in the air.

"Just watching for now," Jane said.

"Have you ever had someone go down on you?" Laura asked as they watched the other man fuck the blonde woman vigorously. He slammed into her, emitting cries of pleasure.

"No," Jane replied. She didn't really know what Laura was talking about, but felt sure that she had never experienced it.

"Shame," Laura said. "You're missing out."

Jane felt a wave of annoyance swell inside her. Who did this woman think she was, judging Jane and laughing at her innocence?

She turned to Laura and said, "Am I? Why don't you

show me then, since you know everything so well?"

She realised she had spoken quite loudly when several people in the room looked their way. She wished the ground would open up and swallow her up. She had been foolish. Laura was probably just making conversation, trying to put her at ease, and she had flown off the handle.

"Very well," Laura replied calmly, much to Jane's astonishment. "Take off your robe and spread your legs."

Jane almost yelped with surprise, but she was also too aroused to say no. She stood up and took off her robe. When she sat back down Laura stood up in front of her.

"Spread your legs," she said, nudging Jane's knee with her leg.

Jane looked around at some of the faces which were now turned her way. If she did as Laura asked, she would be fully on display. To her shock, she found that rather than repel her, this turned her on even more. She inched forward on the sofa and spread her legs. Her cunt throbbed and the coolness of the air on it made her moan with pleasure. She felt equal parts shame and excitement at being ordered around by Laura in front of all these people. She was happy it was a stranger doing this; she would not have to face her again after tonight.

"Look at this beautiful cunt," Laura said to the room at large. A number of people had stopped what they were doing and were now standing in a semi-circle around Jane and Laura. "Can you believe it has never had the pleasure of being licked?"

The people around her didn't laugh and Jane felt another rush of excitement. This was a game, one everyone was used to, and they would not laugh at her.

Laura bent over and whispered. "You asked for this, but you can stop it at any time. All right?"

Jane felt a rush of gratitude. "All right. But please don't hold back."

Laura grinned and straightened up. Jane wondered what had made her so bold, so reckless. She didn't know

Laura, didn't know what she would do. But she wanted to be teased, yes, humiliated even. She loved hearing Laura talk about her to her audience. She loved having an audience for this.

Laura knelt between Jane's legs and spread them wider. She used her fingers to spread Jane's inner labia and slid her fingers through them. Jane whimpered softly.

"Look at how wet this little slut is," Laura said, holding up her hand for her audience to see. "I think I'll need to give her a proper fucking."

"Oh yes," someone muttered in the crowd.

"I'll need someone to take care of those perky little breasts as well," she called out. "Do I have a volunteer?"

To Jane's delight the person who stepped forward was Lillian. She knelt next to Jane on the sofa and kissed her forehead. "Are you all right?" she asked.

Jane grinned. "Never better."

Lillian nodded, then reached out and pinched Jane's nipples hard. Jane gasped at the stinging sensation, but the next moment, Lillian's mouth was on her nipple, licking and sucking. The feeling was exquisite and Jane felt her body become weightless with pleasure.

Laura focused her attention back to Jane as well. She bent down and the next moment Jane felt her tongue slide over her hot cunt. Laura curved her tongue to tease the entrance to Jane's cunt and then licked her clit. Jane moaned and bucked, but Laura held her firmly in place. Through half-closed eyes Jane watched the people around her. Some of the men were stroking their cocks and two women had their hands between their legs, rubbing lazily as they watched her. She felt sexier than she ever had in her life, powerful despite being subjected to Laura and Lillian's whims. Knowing that her pleasure aroused the people around her served as an extra stimulus.

Laura's tongue did not let up on her cunt. She felt the tension build in her body; her legs stiffened as wave after wave of pleasure crashed over her, bearing her higher with each hit, but never quite pushing her over the edge. She moaned and writhed, drifting into her own world of pleasure. Suddenly Laura stopped and Jane's eyes snapped open. She had not reached her orgasm yet. Why did Laura stop?

Lillian stopped as well and she looked up. Jane exchanged a glance with her, but Lillian's face did not reveal anything.

"So close to coming," Laura said, her voice purring. "So wet and hot and delicious. But I think she needs something inside that greedy cunt of hers. She needs to be filled up."

Jane struggled to sit up. She did not want a strange man entering her, if this was what Laura was asking. Lillian gently pushed her back down onto the sofa with a reassuring smile. A number of men in the audience moved forward as if to volunteer, but Laura laughed.

"No, boys, this is between us ladies. You have the pleasure of watching. I have enough here to work with." She reached over and picked something up from the sofa, next to Jane. She held it up for her to see and arched her eyebrows. Jane saw with relief that it was a dildo, bigger than the one Lillian had used on her, but nevertheless a reassuring sight. She nodded to Laura and Laura held it up in the air.

"Now this is something I can work with," she said to the cheers of the bystanders. "Let's see if this little slut can accommodate Mr Big here."

Several people crowded forward to get a better look. Lillian returned to licking and rubbing Jane's nipples and Jane relaxed. Laura rubbed the dildo through Jane's slit, coating it in her juices.

"Here we go," Laura called out and positioned the cock at Jane's entrance. She started pushing and Jane gasped. It was significantly bigger than the one Lillian had used, even bigger than Sidney's cock, and she felt her cunt stretch impossibly. Laura started rubbing Jane's clit and spasms of electricity run through her.

"She's very good," Laura said, "look how well she stretches. She is tight, but she can take this big cock just fine. Doesn't that feel nice and full, darling?" she added to Jane.

"Oh yes," Jane moaned, panting.

"Just a little bit more," Laura said, just as Jane thought she couldn't possibly be filled up more. Laura continued strumming Jane's clit which made all the difference. She could feel her vaginal walls contracting against the huge dildo inside her and she knew she was close to an orgasm.

There were some gasps from the audience as Laura pushed the dildo all the way inside Jane. "Let's leave that in place for now," Laura said, stepping back and looking down on her. "Her cunt looks stunning, doesn't it?"

Jane looked around. Some of the men were rubbing their cocks hard and she could see the tips of some of them wet with their fluid. One of the women had taken out a dildo of her own and was thrusting it hard into her cunt, her eyes riveted on Jane's. Jane felt exhilarated. She was stretched out, on display and the object of lust for all these people and it felt glorious. She had never felt so hot in her life. She pushed against the dildo inside her, eager for Laura to thrust. The clitoral stimulation felt amazing, but she wanted more.

"Fuck me," she panted at Laura.

"Excuse me?" Laura said. "What was that?"

Abandoning all decorum, Jane cried out, "Please fuck me, Laura."

There were several gasps around the room and Laura laughed. "Look at how wanton my little fuck slut has become," she said. "Well, I'll have to give her what she wants, won't I?"

Jane saw Lillian eye her with concern, but she was past caring. She wanted to be fucked, used, displayed, and she didn't care who did it.

Laura didn't waste time. Seizing the dildo in one hand

while still working Jane's clit with the other, she pulled the big shaft almost all the way out before slamming it back into her. Jane cried out in passion, bucking her hips to meet the dildo at the same rhythm. Lillian kissed her nipples, her neck, her face and Jane let herself be carried on the tide of her wantonness, the tension inside her body building to impossible heights until, finally, the dam broke and she came harder than she ever had. She cried out and felt a gush of liquid spill out of her when Laura withdrew the dildo. She heard gasps from around the room and thought she saw one or two of the men ejaculate, but she was too far gone. Lillian cradled her, whispering sweet nothings in her ear while Laura kissed and licked Jane's swollen and abused sex. Finally Jane came down from her orgasm and the crowd around her dispersed. Laura and Lillian helped her sit up and pull her kimono around her.

"Are you all right?" Lillian asked.

Jane shook herself, as if coming out of a daze. "I think so," she mumbled.

"You were fabulous," Laura said, kissing Jane's forehead.

Lillian put her arm around her. "Do you want me to take you upstairs?"

Jane didn't know what she wanted. She felt amazing, but strangely detached from reality. She wanted to hang on to her high, but she also felt as if all eyes in the room were on her.

"I need some air," she said.

"I'll take you outside." Lillian took her arm and helped her up off the sofa.

Jane was dimly aware that she should say something to Laura, but words failed her. She nodded vaguely to the woman who had, minutes ago, given her so much pleasure. Laura smiled and brushed her cheek. Lillian led her to the door. On the way out, Jane spotted Sidney. She almost stumbled when she saw him, his gaze on her inscrutable. Then Lillian pulled her through the door.

CHAPTER 11

Her legs shaky and hardly able to carry her, Jane followed Lillian to the garden where they sat down on a bench. She shivered even though the evening air was still warm. Lillian drew her into a hug.

"How are you feeling?"

Jane laughed shakily. "I'm not sure. I feel satisfied, but my legs are all wobbly."

"You were fantastic," Lillian said, but Jane caught an undertone in her voice.

"But what?" she demanded.

"Nothing."

"I can tell you have reservations, tell me."

"I don't have reservations," Lillian said. "I'm just worried about you."

Jane sat up straighter. "You don't need to be worried about me. I'm fine. I knew what I was doing and I got what I wanted."

Lillian put a hand on Jane's cheek. "I know, but sometimes this kind of play can be overwhelming. Putting yourself on display like that...it's not for the faint hearted."

Jane opened her mouth to refute Lillian, but then thought better of it. She did feel shaken, and it wasn't all because she had had an amazing orgasm. Being on display, that is exactly what she had been. It was what she had wanted, but she couldn't deny that reality was setting in. She had been on display – not only in front of a whole crowd of strangers, but also in front of Sidney. What would he think of her? Now that she had given herself over so freely to a complete stranger? She likely would never meet this Laura again, yet she had been fine with this woman opening up her cunt with her fingers, displaying her wantonness to the whole room and fucking – yes fucking, because that was what it had been – her senseless. Everyone in the room had been able to see Jane's exposed cunt, her legs twitching as she came, her fluids spilling out of her. And the words she had moaned in her ecstasy. Jane buried her head in her hands when it all came back to her. She had been so vile, ready to be taken by anyone. Ready to have a big dildo shoved in her hot, wet hole for everyone to see.

"What have I done?" she whispered.

Lillian stroked her hair. "You haven't done anything," she soothed. "You just had a bit of fun. Intense, earth-shattering fun, but no harm was done."

Jane looked up. "A bit of fun? I was fully exposed to everyone in the room, being fucked by a woman I 've never met."

"And you loved every minute of it," Lillian reminded her. "Every glorious, pleasure-soaked minute. Don't let guilt or shame drag you down, baby. Remember how amazing it felt."

Jane could feel the arousal building in her belly again, thinking about the pleasure she had had. But the shame was there as well, turning her arousal bitter. "What's wrong with me?" she asked. "Why did that make me feel so good? What kind of pervert am I?"

"You're not a pervert." Lillian pulled her to her soft and yielding bosom. "You're just a girl being let off the leash, finding her way in the world. You've been suppressed for too long and now you're getting a taste for whatever else is out there. And Rachel's parties are the best place to enjoy yourself like this and experiment a bit. It's a safe place and no one will breathe a word of this outside the party."

Jane's breath slowed down and she rested her head on Lillian's chest. Lillian smelt heavenly and her voice soothed her. "What about Sidney?" she said.

She felt Lillian stiffen for a moment. "Sidney? What about him?"

Jane sat up and looked at Lillian. "He was there too. He was watching me."

"And he probably loved every minute of it," Lillian said. "Why is that such an issue?"

"Well, I don't have to see any of the others tomorrow, but how can I face Sidney?"

Lillian laughed. "How can you not? Sidney is not a prude himself. He has been to far more of these parties than you have. He can't judge you."

"I don't think he ever joins in though," Jane said. "And here I am joining in on my first party."

Lillian's expression darkened. "He can't judge," she repeated. "If he stood there looking at you being fucked, he likely got off on it. Whether he engages in sex at the parties or whether he enjoys watching, then going to his bedroom and frigging himself is not really different, is it? He joined in just as much as you, even if he wasn't on display himself."

Jane sighed. "You really think so?"

"Yes, I really think so. Don't worry so much about what Sidney thinks. You don't have the same worries about me or Rachel."

Jane hugged Lillian. "You were there, so I knew you didn't judge me. And Rachel hosts these parties; I wouldn't expect her to be judgmental."

"And Sidney happily attends them."

Lillian had a point. Jane leaned against her again. She

was starting to feel sleepy and wished for her bed.

"Do you want me to take you upstairs?" Lillian asked, as if reading her mind.

Jane nodded. "Do you mind?"

"Not at all."

Lillian helped Jane to her feet. Jane winced. Her cunt felt sore, although it was a pleasant reminder of what had happened to her in the last few days.

"Sore?" Lillian asked.

Jane nodded.

"I have something that can help with that. I'll take you to your room and then get the ointment."

They walked towards the house. Jane spotted Matthew at the other end of the patio. He leaned against the wall smoking a cigarette. He was still fully dressed. He clearly had not participated in tonight's activities. Jane's heart went out to him. Perhaps Richard hadn't shown up after all.

Lillian led Jane up the stairs and left her in her room. Jane let the kimono fall to the ground and crawled onto the big, soft bed. She sighed with contentment. It had been a good day, and an even better evening.

A knock on the door announced Lillian's return and Jane called for her to enter. Lillian joined Jane on the bed.

"Okay, spread your legs."

Jane obeyed. Lillian caressed Jane's swollen cunt, her cool hands soothing. Jane moaned with delight. She could feel the wetness gathering again, despite being exhausted. She slowly pushed her hips higher to meet Lillian's fingers, trying to get a bit more pressure.

"You've had quite enough," Lillian said with a chuckle as she pulled her fingers away. "You need sleep and you need to give your poor sex a rest. I'm sure we can play again tomorrow."

Jane groaned, but didn't argue. She was tired and the thought of more pleasure the next day made her happy. There was no rush. She wasn't going home anytime soon.

Lillian covered her up and kissed her. She quietly left the room.

Jane felt her eyes grow heavy, the lure of sleep beckoning. A sharp knock on the door jolted her out of her slumber though. Before she could call "enter", the door opened and Rachel came in. Jane propped herself on the pillows and looked at her friend in the semi-darkness.

"Where were you tonight?" She didn't recall seeing Rachel anywhere once the party had started.

Rachel smiled. "I was in my room, I had a guest to entertain."

Intrigued, Jane leaned forward, her sleep forgotten. "A guest? I take it they wanted to remain anonymous."

"They did," Rachel confirmed.

Jane noted how Rachel didn't reveal the sex of her mystery guest. She decided not to pry. If Rachel felt it important to shield the identity of her lover, she must have had a reason.

"I hope you had fun," she said instead.

"And more to come." Rachel winked. "I just wanted to check up on you."

"Oh?"

Rachel's expression turned serious. "I talked to Lillian. She told me about your experience tonight."

Despite herself, Jane felt her cheeks redden. "It was an interesting experience."

Rachel took Jane's hand. "Something like that can be very intense. Are you sure you're all right? If I'd known what you'd been planning tonight, I would've made sure to be there."

Rachel's tone was full of concern, but she didn't sound patronising. Jane smiled warmly. "I'm fine. Yes, it was intense, but in a good way. Lillian was there and she took care of me." Rachel winced and Jane pressed her hand. "Really, Rachel, don't worry. I was in good hands."

"I should've been there," Rachel murmured. "I fear I've left you alone too much."

"You haven't," Jane insisted. "I haven't felt neglected for a minute."

Rachel leaned over and kissed Jane on the cheek. "I'm glad you feel that way. You and Lillian seem to get on quite well."

Jane could feel her blush deepen. "Yes, we do."

She yawned. The events of the night were catching up with her and sleep once more tried to claim her.

"I'll let you rest," Rachel said. "Please do come talk to me if things get too much for you."

Jane hugged her. "I will. Thank you for checking up on me."

Rachel got up from the bed. "Good night, Jane."

"Good night."

As the door closed quietly behind Rachel, Jane's eyes closed.

CHAPTER 12

It was another hot day and Jane and Lillian had retreated into the shade at the edge of the sprawling garden. Jane's cunt was still sore from the night before, but it was not unpleasant. The occasional tingle invoked nice memories. Lillian lay on her back, one hand resting on Jane's thigh, lightly caressing her.

Sidney appeared around the brush and stopped dead in his tracks when he saw them. Jane shot up, her heart pounding. For a moment Sidney looked like he was going to turn around and walk away, but then he gingerly approached them.

"Join us," Lillian called out when she spotted him. "It's lovely in the shade."

Sidney sat down, but avoided Jane's eye. Jane felt a blush creep along her face. She had a feeling that he was annoyed at her, and she could guess why. He had seen her at the party, and he was disappointed that she had let another woman – a stranger no less – defile her. She didn't know what to say to him and she plucked at her dress in order to avoid his eye.

"Did you have fun at the party last night?" Lillian asked him brightly, and Jane could have kicked her. Why would she bring that up?

"It was nice," Sidney said tersely.

"I saw you watching Jane. Didn't she put up a good show?" Lillian continued.

Jane wanted to sink into the ground. She did not want to talk to Sidney about that.

Sidney made a strangled noise and Jane looked up. He was beet red and glared at Lillian, who smiled sweetly at him.

"It…eh…" he stammered.

Lillian narrowed her eyes at him. "You didn't like it?" she asked. "I thought you were into such things. I always see you watch the public humiliation scenes with much interest."

Jane knew she was teasing Sidney, and she wanted to tell her to stop. She didn't want Sidney to say he was repulsed by what she had done; it was plain to read from his face.

Sidney cleared his throat and avoided looking at Jane. "It was fine," he said.

"Fine?" Lillian would not let go and Jane wanted to run away and hide. "I thought it was incredibly hot. Jane is practically a virgin, but gave herself completely to a strange woman. It was brave and probably the sexiest thing I've seen in a long time. And you call it fine?" She scoffed. "There's something wrong with you."

"Okay, it was hot." Sidney's face had taken on a dark red hue. He avoided looking at Jane. "It was unbearably hot and I wanted to participate. There are not many women who are comfortable being humiliated like that and I didn't think Jane had it in her."

Jane froze. Sidney was not disgusted by what she had done; on the contrary, it had aroused him. Her heart suddenly felt lighter. She reached out her hand to Sidney.

"You're not mad?" she asked.

Sidney caressed her hand. "Mad? Why would I be mad?"

"Because I was so brazen, and I allowed myself to be invaded like that."

He leaned over and kissed her. "What you do is your business. Even if I didn't like a woman who isn't afraid to show herself to a room full of strangers, I wouldn't have any right to be mad at you."

Lillian kissed Jane's neck. "See? There was no reason for you to be so worried yesterday. Turns out our Sidney likes his girls slutty. He clearly loved seeing you so filthy."

Slutty. Filthy. Jane would never have guessed that she would become aroused hearing herself described like that. And yet, there was no mistaking the throb in her cunt.

"I must admit I'm relieved," she said with a smile.

"Seeing you enjoy yourself like that was very arousing," Sidney said, his voice hoarse with lust. "You've come a long way, Jane."

Yes, she had. And she loved every minute of it.

Before she could answer, Rachel and Matthew appeared in their midst. Matthew's eyes looked puffy and Jane wondered if he had been upset about Richard's absence the night before. Rachel's hand rested on his back. Jane wasn't sure whether to show concern for Matthew or to pretend she didn't notice his upset look. Was he staying at Rachel's because he had problems with Richard? Or was there more between him and Rachel than friendship?

"There you are," Rachel exclaimed. "We've been looking for you."

"And you've found us," Lillian said. "Please join us."

Rachel shook her head. "I'm bored of being at home. Matthew and I are going for a drive, do you want to come?"

"Not me," Lillian said. "It's too hot to be in the car."

"I'll go." Sidney got to his feet. "Will you come, Jane?"

Jane shook her head. She agreed with Lillian: it was too hot to be going for a drive. She wanted to stay in the shade, relax a little.

"I'd rather stay here," she said.

Sidney looked disappointed, but he quickly wiped the expression off his face.

"Are you sure?" he asked.

"Yes, it's too hot for a drive. The shade is a much better place to be on a day like this."

"You can stay with us," Lillian said, the implication clear in her voice.

Jane's heart flipped at the idea of spending an afternoon with Lillian and Sidney. Sidney looked tempted, but then shook his head.

"No, I'll go with Matthew and Rachel," he said.

"Suit yourself," Lillian said cheerfully. "See you later."

Jane could not deny the pang of disappointment as she watched him walk away.

It was the perfect afternoon. It was quiet in the garden with only the sound of insects buzzing in the nearby flowers. The servants would be in the house, escaping the hot weather and cleaning up after the party. Lillian lay back on the blanket, her knees drawn up. She seemed oblivious of the fact that her panties were fully visible, her dress bunched up around her waist. Jane couldn't keep her eyes away. Lillian's legs were slightly parted and Jane could see a patch of wetness on the cream satin. Heat gathered between her thighs when she imagined herself stripping Lillian's panties off, and burying her nose in Lillian's cunt. She had been passive in her sexual exploits so far. While she had enjoyed being told what to do, being used and fucked, she suddenly wished she was the one doing all the fucking. Not only that, she wanted to see Lillian at the height of her climax – a climax brought on by her. She had wanted to explore Lillian's cunt for days, and now that the opportunity was finally here she could not resist.

Arousal, never far beneath the surface, bubbled up in her and she looked around. They were outside of the view of the house, quite alone in the garden. No one would notice if she and Lillian would start something. Rachel, Matthew and Sidney were not likely to be back soon, and even if they did... Jane suppressed a shiver of excitement. Knowing that there was a chance of being seen, being discovered, heightened her excitement for ravishing Lillian.

She moved closer. She rested her hand lightly on Lillian's knee and looked at her to gauge her reaction. Lillian's eyes were half closed, but her breath hitched when Jane slowly moved her hand lower, down her thigh towards the patch of wet fabric. Lillian spread her legs slightly wider and Jane trailed her fingers over the wet patch, pressing down slightly. Lillian moaned and lifted her hips, pushing her cunt against Jane's hand. Jane felt like she could barely breathe. She wanted to rip off Lillian's panties and bury her head there, licking and fingering and feasting on her cunt, but she forced herself to take it easy. She remembered how much better it had felt when Lillian had forced her to wait.

Lillian lifted her hips higher in a clear invitation and Jane sat up next to her. She hooked her fingers under the waistband of Lillian's panties and pulled them down her legs. Lillian sighed as she let her knees fall on either side. Jane swallowed when she got her first good look at Lillian's cunt. She knelt between Lillian's legs and, using her fingers, she spread Lillian's outer labia apart. Lillian moaned, but Jane was determined to take it slow. She wanted to savour her first experience of pleasuring another woman.

Apart from her first time with Lillian, Jane had never taken a good look at her own cunt. What she remembered from the night with Lillian were delicate folds of pink flesh between a mass of dark curls between her legs. Lillian kept the hair between her legs trimmed and her inner lips stuck out from her outer labia. The flesh was just as delicate, but a darker shade of pink. Jane trailed her fingers between the wet folds and Lillian moaned again, thrusting her hips up against Jane's hand.

Jane lifted her wet hand to her lips and licked off Lillian's juices. She looked at Lillian as she did so, pushing each finger between her lips and sucking the juice off completely, savouring the acrid taste. Lillian's eyes widened and she licked her own lips.

"Don't tease me." Lillian's voice sounded hoarse.

"Patience," Jane said. "Doesn't it feel a lot better when you have to wait for it?"

Lillian's dark eyes were even darker with desire.

"I want to taste you, bury my fingers deep inside you and explore your cunt," Jane said. Lillian gasped and Jane's cunt throbbed at the sound. "I'm going to eat you out and make you climax hard." Jane didn't even know where the words came from. She only knew that saying them made her wet and she could see that her words had the same effect on Lillian.

She trailed her fingers lazily through Lillian's slit, while looking at her face. "I'm the one in charge now," she told her, "but I promise you I will make you come. After all, I've learnt from the best."

Lillian grinned, perspiration forming on her upper lip. "Don't tease me too long," she said. "Or I may not be able to wait patiently."

Jane smiled, then turned her attention again to Lillian's sex. She bent closer, her nose almost touching Lillian's cunt. She breathed in the smell of her desire, similar, yet different from her own. She parted Lillian's inner lips and felt for her hot core. Lillian was wet, her desire dripping out of her, staining the blanket. Jane slid her fingers from Lillian's entrance up towards where Lillian's clit was hiding under its hood. She pulled back the skin slightly and flicked the exposed clit with her finger. Lillian moaned and rocked her hips.

Jane didn't hesitate any longer. She lowered her head and slid her tongue over Lillian's wet sex. Lillian moaned as soon as Jane's tongue made contact and this spurred her on. With the point of her tongue she probed Lillian's cunt lips apart, lapping at the juices within. She slid her tongue through Lillian's sex, all the way up to her clit. Lillian's clit fascinated Jane: it seemed to play hide and seek, peeking out from under the hood and then disappearing again. Jane flicked it with her tongue, then pressed harder when Lillian moaned louder. The cute bud seemed to swell underneath her tongue until it was no longer able to hide.

Lillian's moans became louder as Jane lavished her attention on her sensitive flesh. She slipped a finger inside Lillian's cunt, feeling the walls pulsate against her. She slid another finger in and curled them up deep inside Lillian. This produced the desired result as Lillian started thrusting her hips against her hand, her juices coating Jane's hand and chin.

Jane's own panties were soaked, but she ignored the throbbing between her thighs. She could get relief later. She wanted to concentrate on Lillian now. She had not realised how amazing it could be to make another person squirm and moan with pleasure and each thrust from Lillian made her more and more aroused. She ground her own sex against the heel of her foot, providing some relief as she continued to lave on Lillian's cunt.

Jane could have spent hours giving Lillian pleasure. The moans and sighs her fingers and tongue elicited were the most beautiful music to her ears. If Lillian would let her, Jane would worship her every day for the rest of her life. Her own pleasure was not as important as Lillian's. Jane couldn't believe how fortunate she was. Lillian buried her hands in Jane's hair and pushed her harder against her sex. Jane's heart filled with love and gratitude. She felt as if she had been chosen; as if Lillian was a priestess and Jane her acolyte. From the pitch of Lillian's moans, she figured Lillian was close to an orgasm and part of her was saddened by this. She didn't want this to end.

Lillian's cunt clamped around Jane's fingers and her moans became shrieks. Jane felt Lillian's belly tighten and suddenly Lillian cried out and clenched her legs tightly around Jane's face. Her fluids gushed into Jane's mouth and Jane drank greedily, delighted she had been able to bring Lillian to this point. Remembering how amazing it felt to be caressed while recovering from her orgasm, she lightly licked Lillian's cunt, her tongue soft and gentle.

After a while, Lillian relaxed. Jane sat up and wiped her chin. She wanted to crawl on top of Lillian and feel her body pressed against hers. But she smoothed Lillian's dress over her knees instead and lay next to her.

"That was amazing," Lillian whispered, a dazed look on her face. "Truly amazing. Thank you so much."

Jane smiled. She felt as satisfied as if she'd had an orgasm herself. "You're very welcome," she whispered back, kissing Lillian lightly.

Lillian threw an arm around Jane and snuggled up to her. Despite the heat, Jane welcomed the embrace. For a while they lay entwined like this, the only sounds the buzzing of the insects and their own heavy breathing.

After a while Lillian snuck her hand down, over Jane's belly and down to her cunt, seeking out the wet heat there. Jane moaned with relief as Lillian slipped her hand inside of Jane's underwear and between her folds. She closed her eyes as Lillian's expert fingers started coaxing her towards her orgasm.

CHAPTER 13

Jane dipped her feet in the water and sighed with relief. The day was hot again and she was happy Rachel had suggested a swim. The others were already in the water, but Jane took her time. She wanted to savour the moment the water engulfed her, cooling her down.

As she waded into the river, her nipples puckered with cold. The water soothed her cunt and for a moment she stood still, savouring the coolness on her swollen sex, but before she could get too aroused, she plunged ahead, submerging in the cool dark. When she came up for air, she had drifted from everyone else. She didn't mind, she wanted some time by herself.

Jane couldn't believe she had only been at Rachel's for two weeks. The shy, inquisitive girl she had been when she had arrived was gone. She no longer hesitated to shed her clothes to go swimming. She grinned. There were a lot of things she no longer hesitated to do.

She floated on her back and looked at the sun-dappled leaves of the trees overhanging the lake. Life was good. The summer was turning out great and she loved every minute she spent with Lillian and Sidney. They were both amazing in their own way. She was surprised she could have such deep feelings for both of them. She had been sure she had wanted to marry Sidney. All her attention had been on him, but she could not deny that Lillian had put her under a spell. She didn't want the summer to end. She didn't want to leave Lillian. It wasn't just that Lillian made her feel so good with her slender fingers and gentle tongue. She was enthralled by Lillian herself. Her husky voice, her soft, yielding flesh. And the way she had taken Jane under her wing. If nothing else, Jane would always be grateful for that. Had it not been for Lillian's guidance, she would never have been bold enough to experience sex.

At the same time a bit of unease crept into her thoughts when she remembered the amazing time she had with Lillian. She loved being with her, but it was something that couldn't last. Lillian would go back to her work after the summer, singing and recording music, and Sidney would go to...where would he go? She realised with a start that she didn't even know where he resided. It must be in the city, but the thought of having to go back there, socialising in the same circles as her Aunt and Uncle did not appeal in the least. Where would that leave her? Who would she go with?

She knew who she wanted to go with, but she had a feeling that it wasn't up to her. Would Lillian really want Jane in her life beyond the summer? Jane felt sure that they had an amazing connection, but would Lillian want it to last beyond these few weeks? Would it even be possible for her to be with Lillian? Marriage was much more stable – at least with Sidney she would be secure. Taken care of.

She sighed and swam a bit closer to the river bank. Maybe she was overthinking things. She would still be at Rachel's for a few more weeks, surely things would work themselves out.

Her feet touched the bottom of the river and she got out of the water. Rachel and Matthew were already unpacking the picnic and Jane joined them.

"Lovely spread as ever, darling," Matthew remarked.

Rachel smiled. "Cook makes an amazing picnic lunch. I had very little to do with it."

Jane sat down on the blanket and popped a grape into her mouth. "Do you never do your own cooking?"

Rachel shook her head. "What's the point if you can have a cook? I don't enjoy it, so why waste my time?"

"Rachel enjoys the easy life," Matthew said. "Not that I blame her."

"You're looking happier." Jane regretted the words as soon as she had said it. Matthew had been moping around the house ever since the sex party, but today he seemed in a much lighter mood. No one had commented on his state of misery and Jane worried she had committed a faux pas.

"I am happier." Matthew did not seem offended at her comment.

"He and Richard have patched things up," Rachel explained. She rummaged in the picnic basket and muttered a curse. "We don't have glasses. I'm just going to get them."

She slipped into her dress and stalked towards the house.

Matthew turned back to Jane. "Sorry I've been so down lately. Rachel's right: Richard and I had a fight. But it's all fine now."

"I apologise, I didn't mean to pry," Janes said.

Matthew waved her apology away. "It's fine. It's not a secret."

Encouraged by his words, Jane continued. "Are you and Richard a couple?"

Matthew shrugged. "Let's just say we like each other's company."

"Also at these parties?"

Matthew busied himself with opening a bottle of champagne. "To be honest, I'd love to participate in the parties, but Richard is less keen. He likes to watch, but he doesn't want to be seen."

Jane frowned. "Rachel's parties are so safe, though. No one would judge him."

Matthew popped the cork and put the bottle of champagne down. "It's not as easy for two men to participate together as it is for two women, or for a man and a woman. What Richard and I do…is illegal. What you and Lillian do is not."

"That doesn't make any sense."

"No, it doesn't. But it is what it is."

"Is that why you're staying with Rachel? To have a safe place for you and Richard?"

A cloud passed over Matthew's face. "Not exactly. My parents found out about my…preference. They cut me off, so Rachel lets me stay with her until I get myself sorted."

"I'm so sorry." A chill took hold of Jane's heart. Sex with Lillian was fun – a lot of fun – but the reality was that a relationship between two women was not accepted in society. It was even worse for Matthew. The consequences of his relationship with Richard would be so much more serious.

Rachel's voice broke the silence. "Why the sombre faces?"

Matthew flashed Rachel a bright smile. "A bottle of champagne and no glasses. But here you are, rescuing us."

Jane took her cue from Matthew and got up to accept a glass from Rachel.

Rachel bellowed from Lillian and Sidney to get out of the water. Laughing together, Lillian and Sidney approached the picnic. A stab of jealousy pierced Jane's heart but she ignored it. She was just being silly. Why shouldn't they have fun?

"So is there a party tonight?" Jane asked as she took a sip of her champagne.

Rachel shook her head. "No, we can't have parties all the time. Besides, we're going out tonight."

"We are?"

"I have to perform tonight, it was arranged before I agreed to spend the summer here," Lillian said. "Rachel has promised that you'll all come and see me."

Jane's heart lifted. She had never been to a night club and to be able to hear Lillian sing was such a wonderful surprise. "That will be lovely! I'm so looking forward to hearing you sing. We'll have so much fun."

She looked at the others and caught Sidney's look of annoyance right before he replaced it with a tight smile. What was he annoyed about? Did he not want to go into the city?

"It's a respectable club," Rachel said, "so we'll all behave."

Matthew laughed. "It will be hard, but I am sure we can manage."

Jane did not want to admit to anyone that she had never been in a nightclub before. She had dressed in a short, sparkly dress with gold sandals and had caught a look of approval from Lillian. She had hoped Lillian would have helped her dress again, but Lillian had stayed in her own room, only coming out shortly before they were about to leave.

Lillian said a hasty goodbye to them all when they arrived at the club, before disappearing backstage. Rachel, Matthew, Sidney and Jane took a table close to the stage and ordered drinks. Jane felt strange. It had been great playing at being grown up at Rachel's house, but she felt out of place in this club. She didn't belong here. She had only pretended to be an adult, but what did she know of the world? What did she know of the circles which Lillian called her home? She had been silly for thinking she could have a future with Lillian. She didn't belong with these sophisticated people, all smoking their cigarettes, drinking champagne and looking incredibly elegant.

Jane stole a glance around the room. Most women were there with men: the men looking very polished and strong, the women resplendent in their beautiful clothes.

"Champagne?"

Jane started and nodded mutely at the waiter who poured her a glass.

"To Lillian," Rachel said.

Everyone toasted Lillian and drank.

"What do you think?" Sidney asked Jane. He studied her over his champagne glass.

"It's all very sophisticated," she answered.

Sidney laughed. "Oh, it just looks like it is. These people are no different from you and me. They are just here to forget their sorrows for a bit and be soothed with nice music."

"Or they're just here to have a good time," Rachel said.

"Or that," Sidney conceded.

"Are you here to forget your sorrows?" Jane asked Sidney. He shrugged and Jane was intrigued. "What sorrows?" she asked.

"Forget it," Sidney replied. "I'm just here to have a good time."

He gave her a smile, but it was the same tight smile she had seen at the picnic. Jane contemplated letting it go, but she was sick of being treated like an ignorant girl.

"You said that everyone is like us: trying to forget our sorrows. You can't just say that and then leave it." She laid her hand on Sidney's arm. "You can talk to me."

Sidney patted her hand in a gesture Jane found irritatingly patronising. "We'll talk later."

Matthew snorted. "Getting Sidney to talk about his feelings is like drawing blood from a stone."

Sidney glared at him, but Jane smiled. "You're going to have fun, though, right?"

Matthew beamed. "Absolutely. I love hearing Lillian sing, her voice is so soothing."

Jane wanted to ask if his good mood had something to do with Richard, but the lights dimmed and a man stepped onto the stage.

"Ladies and gentlemen, the moment you have been waiting for is here. Please welcome Lillian Smith to the stage."

Everyone applauded and then Lillian walked on to the stage. Jane clapped louder than anyone else. Her face felt warm at the thought that but a few days ago she had been between this woman's legs, fucking her with her tongue and fingers and that Lillian had returned the favour. Then Lillian started to sing and Jane forgot everything. She sat riveted, her hands clasped in her lap while Lillian's voice carried her away. She looked at the beautiful woman on stage, commanding everyone with her voice, transforming a dark nightclub into the most wonderful place on earth. Her chest felt tight while at the same time she felt weightless. Suspended in a world of beauty and love. She drank in the view of Lillian in her shimmering gown, her pale skin glowing, a mysterious smile on her lips. The room was completely silent until the end of the song.

Lillian lowered her head as she sang the last notes, almost too soft to hear over the low music. For a moment the room was in complete silence, then the applause shattered the moment. Jane clapped as loudly as everyone else and for a moment she thought Lillian looked directly at her. Her heart swelled with pride for this woman, but at the same time she felt unworthy of her love. What had happened between her and Lillian could never last beyond the summer. Jane knew that now. This moment served as a stark reminder of how different she and Lillian were.

The music turned upbeat and Lillian took up a faster-paced song. People got up to dance and talking resumed. The spell was broken and Jane felt dejected.

"She's amazing, isn't she?" Sidney asked, his lips close to her ear.

Jane nodded, not trusting her voice. She took a sip of champagne in an effort to compose herself.

"Do you want to dance?"

Jane nodded again and let Sidney lead her to the dance floor. Her heart wasn't in it, but she let Sidney swirl her around, her feet finding the right patterns on their own. Sidney was a good dancer and Jane found it hard not to be uplifted by the music and the movements of her feet. Sidney grinned at her as he swung into a complicated spin which she executed perfectly. She grinned back, feeling that not all was lost. She may not have been in Lillian's league, but Sidney was here, paying attention to her and making her feel special. She had been wrong to think she could have a future with Lillian. Her future was with Sidney. She could marry him and lead a comfortable life.

After a while her feet started to hurt and Sidney led her back to the table. She sunk gratefully down on the chair. Rachel and Matthew were still on the dance floor, performing a complicated dance with perfection. They were a striking pair and if one didn't know any better, one could believe they were a couple. Jane noticed how Matthew's eyes roved the dance floor each time he spun Rachel around though. She followed his gaze, trying to see if she could spot Richard. She didn't see him, and after the next dance Rachel and Matthew joined them at the table.

"What an amazing night." Rachel fanned herself and took a sip of champagne. "I'm so glad we came out."

"Me too." Matthew sounded absent minded as he continued to scan the club. Suddenly he sat up straight and took a large gulp of champagne. He hastily got up. "Excuse me," he murmured before disappearing into the crowd.

Jane smiled as she watched him approach Richard. He took the other man by the arm and led him away.

"Another dance?" Sidney asked.

She turned towards him. Her feet were still sore, but the night wasn't over and she was determined to have a good time. "Why not?"

Jane tried to see Matthew and Richard as Sidney led her to the dance floor, but she failed to do so. She turned her attention back to Sidney as he led her into another complicated dance.

CHAPTER 14

They arrived back at Rachel's house far after midnight. Lillian had stayed behind, catching up with friends. She had ensured Rachel that she would be able to get a ride back to the country the following morning.

Jane didn't want the evening to end. She and Sidney had danced all night, pausing only to refuel on champagne. She felt light-headed and her dark mood from earlier in the evening had lifted.

"What an amazing night." Rachel sank into one of the chairs in the hall and kicked off her shoes. "I had so much fun."

"Me too." Matthew was grinning from ear to ear and Jane couldn't help but wonder what he and Richard had been up to. She was happy he had had a good night too.

"Night cap anyone?" Rachel asked. "Or is it time for bed?"

"I think I've had enough fun for tonight," Matthew said. "I need my beauty sleep."

Rachel grinned up at him. "I'm sure you have."

Her tone was full of insinuation confirming for Jane that Matthew and Richard had done more than just dance that evening.

"I think I may go to bed too," she said. She did not feel sleepy, but she hoped to be able to have some time alone with Sidney.

"You're right, it is quite late." Rachel stood and stretched. "I'll see you all in the morning." She ascended the stairs, followed by Matthew.

Jane stood undecided for a moment, then walked towards the staircase as well. Sidney followed her and they climbed the stairs in silence. At the top Sidney took her hand.

"It was a lovely night," Jane remarked as they slowly walked towards her room.

"It was," Sidney agreed.

He was so close to her, she could feel his body heat. She wanted to bury her face in his chest, drink in his scent, and feel his arms tight around her. She didn't do any of that, though. She wasn't sure what Sidney felt about her; his behaviour the last few days had confused her.

They paused outside of her room. She didn't want Sidney to leave, but she didn't know how to tell him to stay. She held on to his hand and reluctantly opened the door. She turned back to Sidney.

"I had a really good night," she said. "Thank you for the dances."

"You're welcome."

He bent down and kissed her lightly on the lips. He drew back and looked at her.

Jane felt deflated. Was that all she was going to get?

"Have a good night." Instead of turning to go, Sidney lingered on her doorstep.

"Was there something else?" Jane asked.

In response, Sidney took a step towards her and drew her into his arms. His mouth found hers and he kissed her hard. It was all the encouragement Jane needed. She wrapped her arms around him and kissed him back, pressing her body against his. If he was surprised by her passion, Sidney didn't show it. He moved Jane into the room and kicked the door shut behind him. They staggered to the bed and Sidney fumbled with her dress. She pushed his hands away and pulled the dress over her head. Sidney gasped when he saw she was completely naked underneath.

"You naughty girl," he said hoarsely.

Jane's cunt flooded with these words. She wanted to be fucked by Sidney – hard and fast, without mercy. Sidney seemed to sense her mood. He grabbed her roughly by the shoulders, turned her around and pushed her down on the bed.

"I think you need to be punished for being so filthy," he growled.

Jane couldn't contain her smile. Sidney was his old self again! Teasingly, she wriggled her butt up into the air.

"I'm such a naughty girl," she said. "What are you going to do to me?"

Sidney grabbed her hips with one hand while sliding his other between her legs. He slipped his fingers through her aching sex and Jane moaned with desire.

"I think you need to be spanked," Sidney said.

Jane's breath hitched. Spanked. She hadn't been spanked since she was a child, but suddenly the image of Sidney behind her, his hand slapping her ass as she writhed on the bed made her wetter than ever. She could feel her juices coating her thighs, her nipples hard with desire.

"Yes, spank me," she breathed.

Sidney was quiet and Jane thought for a moment that she had ruined the moment. Then his hand connected with her ass, the slap loud in the quiet night. She squealed despite herself, the sting burning more than she had expected. Immediately his hand was back, stroking and soothing.

"Again," she moaned.

Sidney didn't hesitate this time and another slap fell on her other ass cheek, followed by his soothing strokes. She pushed herself further into the mattress so her ass was higher in the air. She did not need to urge Sidney again. He slapped her again and again, pausing less often until Jane felt like she would explode from the burn on her ass alone.

Then it was over and she felt Sidney's lips caressing her sore skin. He licked her abused flesh and Jane moaned. Her cunt throbbed, aching to be filled, but Sidney ignored it for a long time. Finally, when he had kissed every inch of her burning flesh, he moved lower towards her sex. He spread her legs further apart and slipped his tongue between her slick folds. Jane could hardly think any more, she was one mess of exposed nerves. Everything felt heavenly: the stinging of her ass, the pressure on her clit, the smooth, strong strokes of Sidney's tongue on her cunt. Pleasure started to build up, but she wanted to be filled.

Again, she didn't have to communicate her wants. Sidney withdrew for a moment and then his hands were on her hips and she felt his hard cock at her entrance. She didn't want to wait any longer and thrust her hips back against his cock. Sidney groaned as he easily slid inside her. His hips chafed her sore ass, but she was beyond caring.

"Fuck me hard," she gasped. "Please."

Sidney grunted and dug his fingers into her hips. He withdrew and slammed back into her, pushing her hard into the mattress. Jane gasped at how deeply he penetrated her. It was such a different sensation from when she had been fucked while lying on her back. She felt like an animal, all instinct and passion. Her nipples rubbed against the bedding and she slipped a hand between her legs to rub her clit. Tension built inside her, winding her up like a coil ready to be sprung. Each thrust of Sidney's cock wound her tighter until she thought she would snap under the tension. She cried out – incoherent cries of passion. She didn't care who'd hear her, all she wanted was for Sidney to push her over that edge.

Then finally the tension snapped when her orgasm overtook her. She convulsed around Sidney's cock, her cunt clamping around him. Lights burst behind her closed eyelids and her body sung with pleasure. She fisted her hands around the sheets in an attempt to ground herself.

Sidney groaned loudly and thrust harder. Jane thought she would pass out from the pleasure, but before she could wind down from her orgasm, she felt herself approaching another climax. She moaned and spread her legs wider to accommodate him even further. Whatever his cock was hitting deep inside her shot sparks of pure electric pleasure throughout her whole body.

"You're so good," Sidney grunted. "I love how tight you are."

His thrusts became erratic and she felt his cock stiffen. This propelled her over the edge again and as her cunt tightened around his cock she could feel a blast of hot liquid inside her. Sidney thrust a few more times, then collapsed on top of her with a sigh.

Jane tried to regain her breath as rivulets of pleasure still coursed through her. Sidney rolled off her and gathered her in his arms. She felt his seed seeping out of her and part of her was sad to lose it. But she had heard horror stories of women getting pregnant before being married, so she knew she should expel all traces of him. Her body felt heavy, like it was sinking into the mattress. She could barely move. The climaxes Sidney had given her had been exquisite. It was nothing like she had ever experienced with Lillian.

Lillian. She suddenly felt a pang of guilt at having slept with Sidney. It had been glorious and she had needed it – a good, hard fuck – but it somehow felt dishonest to Lillian to have had sex with Sidney while she was away. And not just ordinary sex. Jane remembered Lillian's words. He clearly liked seeing you so filthy. Filthy was exactly the word to describe how she had been tonight. There had been nothing tender in their relations. She had offered herself up to Sidney and the result had been animalistic. And yet…she felt sated and content. Happy even.

She snuggled up to Sidney. He kissed the top of her head. She remembered their conversation from earlier in the evening.

"So were you able to forget your sorrows tonight?" She held her breath as soon as the words had left her mouth. Would this ruin the mood?

Sidney laughed. "You won't let it go, will you?"

"We don't have to talk about it," she said quickly. "I don't know why I brought it up. I just feel that we hardly know each other."

"What are you talking about? We've known each other since we were kids."

"But we've been apart for years and we've lost touch. Last time we spoke you were off to study law. Did you become a lawyer?"

Sidney sighed. He loosed his arms around her and propped himself up on his elbow. "Yes, I became a lawyer. Just like my dad."

Jane wasn't sure what to say, so she merely nodded.

"I didn't want to become lawyer. But Dad can be very persuasive."

Jane remembered that Sidney had always been in awe, if not in fear, of his father. It didn't surprise her that he would have followed in his father's footsteps.

"What would you have liked to become?" she asked, copying his position so she could look at him.

"I don't know. I don't mind being a lawyer, but I don't like working with my father. I think he defends the wrong people."

"Don't lawyers defend all people?"

"Sure, but I would rather defend the poor who don't have much defence of their own. I don't want to defend rich people who can easily afford to treat the poor better."

Jane trailed her fingers over Sidney's chest. "So you want to be a hero."

Sidney frowned. "No, I want to see justice done in the world and I don't see that in my father's practice."

She leaned over and kissed him. "Why don't you go away from him then? Leave the city and start your own practice in the country. It's so lovely out here and you would be away from the influence of your father."

"I should. I want to, but every time I come close to telling my father, the courage escapes me. Besides, I have no money. My father wouldn't support me if I struck out on my own and poor clients don't exactly pay well."

"You need a rich wife," Jane joked.

Sidney's face fell. "Don't say that."

"I'm sorry."

"My father is always trying to marry me off to one of his wealthy friends' daughters. That's partly the reason I came here, to have some respite."

"And to have sex with young, unsuspecting girls?"

Sidney laughed. "You might be young, but you are not unsuspecting. I think you took the initiative tonight."

There was no arguing that and Jane smiled. Sidney kissed her, his tongue probing deep inside her mouth and a moan escaped her. He pushed her down onto the bed and she willingly spread her legs for him again, eager to be satisfied again. As he kissed his way down to her aching sex, she smiled happily.

CHAPTER 15

Jane woke from a delicious dream. She dreamt that she was the centre of attention at one of Rachel's party, men and women alike stroking her, kissing her, fucking her. She could still feel their fingers on and in her cunt, drawing out her desire.

She sighed with disappointment as she woke up, naked and alone. The room was still dark, but the grey light of the early morning peeked through the cracks between the curtains. She reached next to her only to find empty space. Had Sidney departed as soon as she had fallen asleep or had he crept out in the early hours of the morning?

She became aware of a soft knocking on the door. Groggily she clambered out of bed and opened the door. Lillian slipped past her into the room.

"Lillian!"

"I couldn't stay away from you." Lillian embraced her and kissed her.

Jane kissed her back, allowing her body to melt against Lillian's. She savoured every contour of Lillian's body pressed against hers. Her heart swelled with happiness at Lillian's words.

Lillian cupped Jane's naked breasts and flicked the nipples with her fingers. The effect was electric: Jane moaned as currents of pleasure coursed to her cunt.

"Were you with Sidney last night?" Lillian asked when they finally broke their kiss.

Jane's face flushed with heat while she tried to formulate an answer. She shouldn't have to be ashamed of having been with Sidney, but she didn't want to offend Lillian either.

"I thought you were out all night," she said evasively.

"It didn't work out," Lillian replied rather cryptically. "Now answer me: did you fuck Sidney?"

While the words were coarse, Lillian's tone was light and Jane could tell she was aroused, rather than angry.

"Yes, I fucked him," she said, matching Lillian's word choice. "He spanked me and then he pushed me on the bed and fucked me from behind."

She could hear Lillian's breath hitch and she knew she had shocked her. It made her feel strangely powerful.

Lillian kissed her again and pushed her onto the bed. Jane willingly spread her legs and Lillian didn't waste any time. She cupped Jane's mound, and slipped two fingers inside her already soaking cunt. Jane sighed with delight as Lillian curled her fingers up, seeking out the perfect spot. Lillian's fingers found their target and Jane groaned with delight. She gloried at how sensitive her cunt still was from the rough treatment Sidney had given her. She arched her back as her belly tightened with pleasure.

"You slut," Lillian said, admiration in her voice. "You couldn't even wait one night without sex. Did he give you what you wanted? Did he fill up that tight cunt of yours with his big cock?"

Jane moaned. She didn't know why Lillian's words made her so hot, but she was close to a climax already and Lillian had barely done anything. She wanted Lillian to keep talking, it drove her wild to hear herself being described like this.

"He did," she gasped. "He filled me up all the way, ramming his big cock deep inside me. Over and over again. He made me climax more times than I could count."

Lillian kissed her neck. Jane could feel her hot breath as she whispered in her ear. "Did you like it when he spanked you? Were you a dirty slut for him too?"

"I loved being spanked. I am a filthy slut and deserve to be punished."

Lillian moaned and Jane realised that this was as arousing for Lillian as it was for her. She rolled onto her side and sought out Lillian's cunt. As she expected, Lillian was naked underneath her robe, wet and hot. Jane wasted no time, but plunged two fingers into Lillian's dripping hole, curling her fingers up like Lillian did inside Jane.

"You slut," Lillian panted. "I will make you come again. And then you'll fuck me until I tell you to stop."

Jane moaned and pressed her hips into Lillian's hand. She felt like her body was on fire. Her sex throbbed with pure, unadulterated lust. Lillian's deft fingers on her clit brought her close to a climax. She was surprised at her raging arousal; after having been thoroughly taken care of by Sidney she thought she would be too tired. But Lillian was intoxicating and she could smell her juices soaking her hand. She wanted to taste them, lick Lillian's folds, seeking out the hot source of her juices. Lillian moaned and slipped another finger into Jane's cunt. That was enough to push Jane over the edge and she clung to Lillian as her cunt convulsed around Lillian's fingers. Her head spun and she breathed hard. Lillian chuckled and withdrew her hand slowly, lingering a moment on Jane's throbbing clit before pushing her fingers in Jane's mouth. Jane licked eagerly, sucking her own juices off Lillian's fingers. When she was done Lillian kissed her deeply.

"Now you service me," she said. "There's a dildo on your night stand, I want you to fuck me as hard as Sidney fucked you."

Jane stilled at these words, her arousal mounting again. She located the dildo in the semi-gloom of the room. She briefly wondered where it had come from. Lillian must have brought it with her when she came into her room. Which meant she was sure Jane was going to fuck her.

"What are you waiting for?" Lillian demanded.

Jane grabbed the dildo. It was thick and long, much longer than the ones she had used before.

"Which end do I use?" she asked.

Lillian giggled and took her dildo from her. "Both ends," she said. She pulled Jane closer. "Spread your legs."

Jane's eyes widened, but she did as Lillian asked.

"Are you good to go another round?" Lillian asked.

The last shred of modesty she still possessed told her to say "no", but her arousal overruled it.

"Absolutely," she said, her voice husky. She was intrigued and wanted to know what Lillian meant to do with this strange dildo.

Lillian rubbed the dildo through Jane's slick sex, coating it in her juices before poising it at her entrance. She shifted closer and pushed the other end of the dildo in her own cunt.

"It's double-ended," she said. "So we can fuck each other."

Jane gasped when Lillian moved closer, the dildo slipping inside her abused cunt. She moaned when she felt the dildo hit the top of her vagina, which was still sensitive from Sidney's hard thrusts.

Lillian pulled her closer, each movement of her hips pressing the dildo harder inside Jane. She gasped and thrust her hips forward. Lillian's thighs were touching hers now, the dildo connecting them cunt to cunt. Despite having been fucked hard by Sidney, Jane wanted this, she craved it. Lillian moved her hips back and thrust forward again. Jane tried to mimic Lillian's movement and after a few tries they found their rhythm.

"That's it, fuck me," Lillian grunted as the dildo slammed into her again. Jane could feel the impact in her own cunt, sending her into a frenzy of desire. Sweat broke out on her whole body, but the slickness of her skin only served to allow Lillian's thighs to slide effortlessly over hers. She reached between her legs and her eager fingers found Lillian's clit. The dildo was big, stretching her cunt tight and her muscles tightened more with each thrust as the tension mounted in her cunt.

Lillian arched her back, a low moan starting in the back of her throat, a sound Jane recognised and which heightened her arousal even more. She thrust harder, the dildo coated in both her and Lillian's juices, sliding in and out of their cunts. Just as she was about to reach the edge of her climax, Lillian stopped and pulled the dildo out of Jane's cunt.

"Turn around," Lillian said harshly. "That's how Sidney fucked you, isn't it?"

Jane nodded mutely.

"Then get on your hands and knees, you slut, and we'll fuck like that as well."

Jane got up on her knees, her legs shaking. She raised her ass in the air and Lillian plunged the dildo deep inside her. Jane moaned as she felt Lillian's ass touching hers. She reached between her legs and found the dildo wedged between them again.

"This is so hot," she panted as Lillian resumed her thrusts.

She thrummed her clit, determined to reach her climax again. She didn't have to work before her orgasm hit her, faster than she expected.

"No stopping," Lillian said, "I don't care if you came; you're not stopping before I'm done."

Jane groaned, but she didn't want to stop. Her cunt convulsed around the dildo, clamping it inside of her as Lillian thrust against it. Each movement sent fresh waves of pleasure through her body and she buried her head in the pillow to stifle her cries. She didn't think she could possibly have another orgasm, but then Lillian screamed, "I'm coming" and Jane fell over the edge again, shaking and crying.

Lillian fell forward on the bed, the dildo slipping outside of her cunt. Jane prised the other end of the dildo from her own tightened sex and curled up on the bed next to Lillian.

Lillian kissed her and slipped her hand between Jane's legs. She cupped her mound gently. "Not too painful?" she asked with concern in her voice.

Jane smiled. "Not too painful, no. Just the right amount."

Lillian lightly caressed her swollen sex. "I'll need to give you a break tomorrow," she whispered. "Make sure you don't allow Sidney anywhere near your pussy either."

Jane smiled. "Jealous?"

Lillian shook her head. "Just concerned for your welfare."

Jane buried her head in Lillian's neck and grinned. Her hesitation over how Lillian felt about her was gone. This had been a delicious start to the day.

CHAPTER 16

Jane closed her eyes and stretched her legs. The sun beat down on her naked skin and she relished in its warmth. Her body was taking on a much darker hue. A few weeks ago she would have been scandalised at the thought of getting a tan on her whole body. And now she was having sex with two of Rachel's friends! She felt a blush creep up her neck at the thought. It seemed like the woman she had been before she had come to Rachel's had completely disappeared. She almost laughed when she recalled how little she had known about sex when she had first arrived. If only she could have known then how intoxicating it could be. Addictive almost.

"Are you coming in?"

She looked up, shielding her eyes from the sun. Lillian stood over her and Jane ignored the twitch in her cunt as she looked up at her lithe body. She had lost track of how many times she had fucked Lillian already, but the sight of Lillian never failed to arouse her. Between her and Sidney Jane was never left unsatisfied.

"No, you go ahead," she said. She saw the brief flicker of disappointment on Lillian's face and almost changed her mind, but then Lillian nodded.

"Suit yourself. You'll regret it."

Jane smiled and watched her walk away. Matthew and Sidney followed Lillian's example and raced each other to the water, their dicks swinging as they ran. Richard, who had come up for the day, followed at a more leisurely pace.

Jane turned and lay on her stomach to give her back a chance to catch some sun. Rachel moved over so she lay next to her.

"So..." she said.

Silence descended after this, but Jane refused to take the bait. If Rachel had something she wanted to ask, she wasn't going to help her along.

"You and Lillian then?" Rachel asked after a while.

"Yes."

"And also Sidney?"

Jane turned her head to look at Rachel. She hadn't thought Rachel would be judgmental, but her tone wasn't completely devoid of feeling.

"Yes, Sidney too."

Rachel laughed. "You're a quick learner."

"I'm just having fun." She hated how defensive she sounded.

"That's good," Rachel said. "You're here to have fun. I'm sorry I didn't prepare you better for what you could expect here. To be honest, I didn't think you'd embrace sex quite the way you have."

Jane laughed. "Neither did I. But I'm absolutely loving it."

"I'm so happy, darling."

They were silent again. From the direction of the lake came the sound of Lillian laughing. Jane couldn't catch what she was saying, but she heard Sidney's voice say something in response. Lillian shrieked and a sound of splashing followed.

"Lillian is amazing," Rachel said.

"She is."

"I'm so happy you two are getting along."

Jane turned and sat up, distracted by the sounds from the lake. In the water, Lillian and Sidney were locked in an embrace, their faces inches away from each other. Jane felt a surge of jealousy. What was going on?

"Sidney and Lillian are very old friends," Rachel said, as if reading her thoughts. "They're very comfortable around each other."

Jane had been aware that Lillian liked men as well as women. She had seen Lillian take an interest in the men during the sex parties even though she hadn't been physically engaged with any of them. It surprised her that Lillian was sexually interested in Sidney though, although Lillian had been more than happy to help Jane with Sidney.

In the water Lillian briefly kissed Sidney, then swam away from him. He laughed and chased after her. Matthew was floating a little further away, seemingly oblivious.

Despite herself Jane was getting wet at the thought of Sidney and Lillian fucking. She would love to witness that. Would Lillian be as dominant with Sidney as she was with her? Or would she be the submissive, offering up her ass to be spanked by him? Would she love being taken from behind by Sidney? Or was she more adventurous in ways Jane could not imagine?

She shook her head to expel the thought. "Lillian is a free woman, she can do whatever she wants."

Rachel lay her hand on Jane's thigh. "Does it bother you that she may have sex with Sidney?"

Jane examined her feelings carefully. While the thought of Lillian and Sidney fucking aroused her, she couldn't deny the spark of jealousy that had been ignited when she had seen Lillian and Sidney embrace.

"A little," she admitted. "But I don't understand why it should. I mean, Lillian didn't mind me having sex with Sidney."

"Who do you fancy more? Lillian or Sidney?"

She knew the answer to that, but she didn't want to admit it to Rachel. "Sidney," she said. "I've liked him for years. And now I can't believe I've been intimate with him."

"So you would like it if he asked you to marry him?"

Her head whipped around and she gaped at Rachel. "What do you mean? Did he tell you he wants to ask me to marry him?"

Rachel shrugged. "He's in need of a wife and he is quite taken by you. I told him to ask you to marry him. It would work for both of you: he will get a wife and you won't have to go back to living with your aunt and uncle. And you did say you like him."

Jane felt a stab of disappointment. Was that all? Sidney needed a wife and she would do? She had hoped she meant more to him. She would have preferred a romantic declaration of love, not this business-like dealing with Rachel.

"If he wants to marry me, why doesn't he ask me himself?"

"He may. I was just speculating aloud. I don't know if he has given it any thought, but it makes sense, doesn't it? You don't want to go back to your aunt and uncle after this summer, do you? Back to the stifling mess that is their house? Back to not having sex at all?"

When she put it like that, it made sense to Jane, although she still didn't like this logical approach to what she has always viewed as a romantic occasion.

"And besides, you do like him and you clearly like having sex with him, so what's the problem?"

The problem is that I'm in love with Lillian, Jane thought, but she held her tongue. What she had with Lillian was just a bit of fun and couldn't last past the summer. Even if Lillian had deeper feelings for her, Jane couldn't envision how they would make a relationship work out in the real world. She would probably be better off hedging her bets on Sidney. If he really did want to marry her, what was holding her back? She could have her fun with both Sidney and Lillian during the remainder of the summer and then marry Sidney and escape with him. She had only had sex with him a handful of times, but it had been good. More than good, in fact. She felt the familiar tug in her lower belly as she remembered how good it had felt when he spanked her. And his cock filling her up, stretching her almost to the point of being painful. She stifled a groan and next to her Rachel chuckled. Jane scoffed, annoyed with herself for getting aroused so easily.

"I'm going for a walk," she said, getting up.

Rachel smiled, but kept silent and Jane stalked off.

Walking along the river calmed her down. She waved at Matthew who was still swimming leisurely. Richard floated a little distance away. Jane smiled. It was lovely to see Matthew so happy.

She couldn't see Lillian or Sidney, but she didn't care. She wanted to clear her head, not think about sex for a while. She had let arousal drive her actions in the last few weeks, abandoning all caution and decency. Jane felt a sliver of guilt when she thought how she had willingly let Lillian and Sidney defile her. Yes, that was the word for it. Rachel could pretend all she wanted that it was natural with her sex parties and swimming naked, but was it really? Was this what Jane's parents had wanted for her? Had they wanted their daughter to be a slut, ready to open her legs for anyone, male or female? Getting wet at the mere thought of sex, her body gushing fluids, eager to be filled, satisfied? Or was her uncle right, and did she need to exercise some self-control? After all, if she did marry Sidney, he would expect her to be a dutiful wife, having sex with him alone. She couldn't run off to attend sex parties then, couldn't have another woman pleasure her, humiliate her in front of a room full of aroused people.

Jane sighed, annoyed with herself as she felt her cunt contract with desire at the memory of her public humiliation. There must be something wrong with her, she concluded. Surely no one thought about sex as much as she. Even Lillian was able to go to work, and hadn't felt the need to join in at every sex party she attended. Sidney was even more chaste – as far as Jane knew he had had sex with only her during his time at Rachel's. Whereas she had taken any and every opportunity to be fucked senseless. No matter how sore she had been the next day, she had willingly spread her legs again and again, ready to be taken and ravished. It wasn't natural, but she couldn't fight it either. Maybe it was simply the effect of having been repressed for so long. Maybe she just needed to get this out of her system. She hoped so, as she didn't think it would be good to carry on like this.

She neared a clumped of trees when she heard familiar voices. She edged nearer and peeked through the trees. She glimpsed Lillian's lush body sprawled on the soft grass. Sidney lay next to her, propped up on his elbow. Jane froze. She knew she should move, make her presence known or move on, but she couldn't tear her eyes away from the couple on the grass. Lillian's legs were spread and Sidney's hand was between her thighs, rubbing her cunt lazily.

"So, how are you enjoying her?" Lillian asked.

"Hmmm... You've done some good work with her," Sidney replied. "She's amazing. I just wish I'd get more time with her."

Lillian chuckled, then sighed as Sidney pushed a finger or two inside of her.

Jane stifled a gasp as she realised he was talking about her. Her cunt ached and she reached down between her legs. She stifled a moan of frustration. Here she was again, letting her arousal get the better of her. But she couldn't help herself. The fact that Sidney and Lillian were talking about her made her throb with lust.

She circled her clit with one finger, occasionally dipping it inside her cunt to draw more of her juices out. She kept her eyes on the writhing form of Lillian on the grass.

"I can't get enough of her," Lillian said, her voice hoarse with desire and pleasure. "Have you spanked her again, or was it just the one time?"

Sidney threw his head back and laughed, the loud sound shocking Jane. "Oh no, not just the one time. She loves being spanked, you should try it sometime."

Jane tried to muster up some feeling of indignation. They were talking about her as if she had no will of her own. As if she was a play thing, existing only for their pleasure. But rather than feeling indignant, she felt more turned on. It made her wet to think that both Sidney and Lillian desired her that much – and that they were willing to share their experiences of her with each other.

"Tell me what you like to do to her," Sidney growled. His cock was rock hard and he positioned himself between Lillian's legs.

Jane lowered herself onto her knees, her legs wide apart and her fingers deep inside her cunt. This was what she had just fantasised about; she wasn't about to miss it.

Lillian gasped as Sidney entered her. "I have a double ended dildo."

"A big one?" Sidney grunted. He slammed into Lillian hard, pushing her further into the grass.

Jane worked her fingers in and out of her cunt, no longer caring about decency. Her juices coated her hand and thighs and she brought her other hand towards her clit.

"Huge," Lillian moaned. "It's amazing to fuck her with a dildo that's also in my cunt."

Sidney merely groaned in response. Jane could feel the tension build in her body, her fingers taking her near the edge of her climax.

"Our cunts slapping together at each thrust," Lillian continued between gasps. "It makes her come hard and fast, maybe because she pictures your cock when I do it."

Jane's cheeks flushed with heat. She did love the double ended dildo, but not because it made her think of

Sidney's cock. She loved how it could give both her and Lillian pleasure at the same time. She loved hearing Lillian's moans as the dildo fucked both of them.

"Oh, yes!" Sidney grunted. "Tell me more."

"She likes it hard, almost rough. And such a tight little cunt, have you noticed how hard she can squeeze?"

Sidney gasped. "Yes, she is so tight."

Lillian moaned and she rubbed her clit furiously as Sidney continued to fuck her relentlessly. "Her cunt is delicious, don't you think? So smooth and slick, always wet, always ready."

"She is one horny little slut," Sidney agreed.

Hidden behind the trees, Jane gasped. She never thought it would arouse her to hear Sidney call her a slut, but it almost pushed her over the edge. She eased off on her clit, not wanting to come before Lillian and Sidney. Her cheeks burned, but she wanted to hear more.

"It's lovely to have such a ready playmate," Lillian continued, her voice hoarse with desire. "I can't get enough of her. And she's eager to please as well, quite skilled with her tongue for a novice."

"Oh fuck," Sidney groaned.

"You really should teach her to suck your cock sometime. I bet she'd be amazing at it. Her hot little mouth around your fat cock…"

Sidney make a sound that was so primal and animalistic, it touched Jane to her core. She watched in fascination as he pulled his cock out of Lillian and sprayed his come all over her breasts and belly. Her own climax overtook her and her cunt contracted painfully hard around her fingers. She heard Lillian's distinct cry of pleasure as she slumped forward, her hand resting between her legs.

She listened to the sounds of the couple at the edge of the river coming down from their orgasm as she recovered herself. Slowly the world swam into focus and she looked at her hands, stained with her juices. She shivered, suddenly feeling cold and exhausted. Had she not just resolved to stop letting her arousal dictate her actions? Yet here she was, on her knees in the dirt, having frigged herself to an orgasm while spying on her friends having sex. While those friends were talking about her.

She lowered her head, a heaviness settling in her body. She waited until Lillian and Sidney had recovered themselves. After they had entered the river and swam back to Rachel, Matthew and Richard, she picked herself off from the ground, rinsed her body in the water and slowly walked back to join the others.

CHAPTER 17

Jane retired to her room for the rest of the afternoon. She changed into a more formal dress, complete with bra and proper underwear and had her lunch brought up to her room. She ate slowly, looking out over the garden where everyone else lounged around. She had mumbled an excuse as soon as she had joined everyone else at the picnic area and had hurriedly pulled her dress over her head. She didn't look at anyone as she pretty much fled back to the house.

It felt strange being fully dressed again. In the last weeks she had followed Rachel and Lillian's example and had forgone a bra and, quite often, also panties. Rachel didn't stand on ceremony and Jane had agreed that she felt much more comfortable without the trappings of her restrictive underwear. But this afternoon she wore it like armour. She needed to ground herself again, remind herself of who she was and where she had come from. Her cheeks burned with shame as she thought about herself frigging and watching her friends fuck. Especially since it had followed so soon after she had determined to lead a more chaste life.

She pushed the plate away and picked up a book. She would act like a proper lady again. She would read, rest a bit, and maybe even write a letter or two, although she couldn't quite think whom she should write the letters to. Maybe she should write to her aunt and uncle, although she didn't even know where they went each summer. They never left a forwarding address and she had never cared to ask. Now she suddenly longed to be back in New York, in the familiar house, her own bedroom. It had been madness to visit Rachel. While her uncle may be a bit too conservative, Jane didn't know whether the all-encompassing freedom at Rachel's house was good for her either. The way she had let her desire take over completely in the last few weeks could not be right.

Jane sighed and put down her book. She was tired and the letters danced in front of her eyes. She made herself more comfortable in the chair and closed her eyes.

A loud knock on the door woke her. She was disoriented for a moment and couldn't recall where she was. The sun hung low on the horizon and her neck felt stiff. She got up from her chair, her clothing uncomfortably restrictive.

Lillian's voice called from outside the door. "Jane, are you in there?"

"I'm coming," Jane said. She wondered how long she had been asleep. Yawning she opened the door where she was met by a concerned Lillian.

"Where have you been?" Lillian pushed into the room and closed the door behind her. "Are you all right?"

Jane followed her into the room and sat down on the sofa. Lillian sat next to her. "When you didn't show up at dinner, we were all worried. Is everything all right?"

"I'm fine," Jane said. She wasn't sure whether she wanted Lillian in her room. She did not want to succumb to her desire for her. She shifted slightly away. "I was tired and must have fallen asleep. What time is it?"

"It's almost nine o'clock. Are you sure you are all right?"

Jane nodded, but Lillian arched an eyebrow.

Jane sighed. "I just needed a break. Just some time for myself."

"You're dressed, were you planning to go anywhere?" Her voice was laced with concern and Jane detected something else as well. Was it fear? She noticed Lillian's hands, clasped tightly in her lap. She felt a flutter of hope in her chest. Why was Lillian so concerned? Was she really worried that she would leave? Did she mean that much to her?

"I'm not going anywhere," Jane said. "I just..."

Lillian looked at her expectantly and Jane felt something give way in her. She needed a friend. She needed someone to talk to, someone who could allay her fears and doubts. She lay back against the cushions.

"I don't know what I'm doing any more," she began. "These past few weeks have been exhilarating and I've had so much fun. But it seems that all I've been able to do, all I've been able to think about since I arrived here, is sex. And while sex is amazing" – she gave a short laugh at the understatement – "I'm not so sure that this is the right way to behave. I know my uncle is far too conservative, so I shouldn't be concerned with how he raised me, but I can't help wondering: am I going too far? I've had sex with you and Sidney. I've let a strange woman fuck me in front of a room full of people. And I loved it. Who am I? Am I nothing more than a common slut? Is there still a way back? I don't even know what I am going to do after the summer. I can't go back to live with my aunt and uncle, I simply can't. But what else can I do?" Her voice rose to a crescendo and she found she was shaking.

Lillian moved closer and took Jane's hands in hers. "Shhh," she said. "You worry far too much. This is just a summer of fun. Don't overthink it."

Jane pulled her hands away. She had thought Lillian would understand, but she only wanted to placate her. "I'm not overthinking it. This is how I feel. Lillian, it can't be normal, the amount of sex I'm having. All I can think of is sex. And if I'm not with you or Sidney, I let my own hands do the work. It's become an addiction. And it scares me, because this summer is going to end. I can't go through life craving sex this much."

"Why not? I do."

"Yes, but..." Jane was going to say But you're a singer, but she knew that wouldn't be fair. Or make sense, really, because Lillian's profession didn't have anything to do with sex.

"Jane, you don't have to go back to your aunt and uncle, and you don't have to stop having sex. Sure, we're all letting loose this summer, because it's our holiday and we want to indulge, but after the summer you can still want sex. You just have to balance it with everything else."

Jane sighed. "Balance it with what? I wasn't exaggerating. It's easy for you to say that I don't have to go back to my aunt and uncle, but where else can I go? I have no money of my own, no skills and no other family."

Lillian opened her mouth as if she was going to say something, then closed it again. "I don't know, baby, but we'll figure something out. By the end of the summer I promise you we'll find a solution so you don't have to go back to your aunt and uncle."

Jane rested her head on Lillian's shoulder. She wanted so much to believe her, but she couldn't see a way forward.

"In the meantime, stop worrying," Lillian said. "You have a healthy appetite for sex, it's not an addiction. There is nothing wrong in indulging in some fantasies while you can. As long as you're having fun and you're not hurting anyone, you can let your desire run wild. That's what being at Rachel's is all about."

A sense of calm descended on Jane. "So I'm not a slut?" she asked.

Lillian chuckled. "You are definitely a slut, but that's not something to be ashamed of. Who cares what anyone else would think; we all think you're amazing."

Jane smiled and sat up. "Thank you for making me feel better."

"Do you want me to help you undress?" Lillian asked.

"No, thank you. I think I'll read a bit and then go back to sleep. I'll see you in the morning."

Lillian nodded and kissed Jane's cheek. "Sleep well."

"Thank you for checking on me," Jane said.

"That's all right."

Jane stayed on the sofa until she heard the door closed. Then she slowly got up and undressed. It felt great to get out of the restrictive clothes again. What had she been thinking? Those clothes didn't make her feel like herself any more than shutting herself away had done. She didn't know who she was anymore, and it was time to face that reality. Or maybe she had never been allowed to be herself.

Jane paced the room, discarding clothes as she walked. Her whole life she had been told what to do, how to feel, and what to think. Her aunt and uncle hadn't encouraged her to think for herself, or to find her own way in life. The first time she was allowed to make her own decisions had been when she had arrived at Rachel's. Was it really that bad that all her decisions had revolved around sex? Sex was at least a positive experience, unlike the doom and gloom that reigned in her aunt and uncle's place. She had never felt as free and uninhibited as she had these past few weeks, and if sex was the result – or the cause, she couldn't decide – was that really a bad thing?

She thought about what Lillian had said: that she was always thinking about sex as well. And yet she had a successful career as a singer. The summer was just an excuse to live to excess. To give in to the urges they all had to curb during normal life. And Lillian was right: summer would come to an end. Everyone would leave Rachel's to go back to their own lives. Why not enjoy it while it lasted? There were only a few more weeks left until the party would dissolve. Did she really want to spend those weeks cloistered in her room?

Jane felt like her head was going to burst. She didn't know the right answer. She only knew that she wouldn't be able to live with herself if she didn't enjoy every minute of this summer with Lillian, and yes, with Sidney. She would worry about the consequences later. Now was the time to enjoy herself.

She smiled, feeling lighter than she had in days and slipped naked under the sheets. She would get a good sleep, then seek out Lillian and Sidney in the morning. As she could feel the tendrils of sleep overtake her she remembered what Lillian had told Sidney about having him teach her to suck his cock. Her cunt flooded at the thought, until another, more delicious, thought presented itself. What if Lillian taught her how to suck Sidney's cock? The idea of both of them sharing Sidney was almost enough to make Jane lose her self-control again, but she pressed her thighs together to alleviate the ache in her cunt and forced herself to endure at least one night without an orgasm. She wanted to prove that she was not addicted.

CHAPTER 18

Jane had planned to seek out Lillian early in the morning, but by the time she woke up the sun was high in the sky. She ate a quick breakfast and joined the others on the lawn. It was another warm day, although not as scorching as the previous weeks had been. There was a promise of rain in the air.

"There she is!" Lillian crossed the lawn to meet Jane. "Are you all right?" she asked in a low voice.

Jane smiled. "I'm fine. I overslept."

The smile of relief on Lillian's face was unmistakable and Jane's heart skipped a beat. She hugged her. "I have a fantastic idea I need to talk to you about," she whispered.

Lillian drew back and looked at Jane. "What idea?"

Jane grinned. "I'll tell you later. But I think you're going to like it." Just the thought of the proposal made her wet again, but she ignored the low ache in her groin.

A blush spread over Lillian's cheeks and Jane wondered if Lillian could read her thoughts. She took Lillian's arm and led her back to the group.

"So what are the plans for today?" she asked when they reached the others.

"We were thinking of going for a drive," Rachel said.

Jane sat down on a lounger, Lillian by her side.

"A drive sounds nice," she lied.

"It's likely going to rain later, so we don't want to be cooped up in the house all day," Matthew explained.

"We don't?" Sidney asked, and he looked at Jane. Jane felt a blush creep up her neck and looked away.

"No, we don't," Rachel said. "Come on, at least it'll get us out of the house for a bit. I'll drive."

A chorus of protests greeted that statement.

"I will drive," Matthew said. "If we allow you to drive, we won't make it back alive."

Rachel laughed. "Fine. I'll get the car around." She got up and disappeared into the house.

Jane looked around. "Did Richard leave yesterday?" She suddenly felt bad that she hadn't come down for dinner. She didn't want Matthew to think she was avoiding him and Richard.

Matthew smiled. "He had to leave this morning, unfortunately. But hopefully he'll be back later."

His obvious joy was infectious and Jane found herself smiling broadly. "I'm so happy."

"Yeah…" Matthew suddenly looked bashful. "It's good to have some time together."

Lillian smacked him playfully on the arm. "And now he's so stir-crazy he wants to take us all out on a drive. Can't sit still until his lover is back."

Jane couldn't blame him. She could barely make it through one day without sex.

"I'll go and see if Rachel needs any help," Matthew said.

"We'll be along shortly," Lillian called after him.

Sidney got up. "We can't really say no to our hostess, can we?"

Lillian laughed and joined him. "No, we can't. I am sure we can hold off a bit longer though. Besides, Jane has an idea." She turned to Jane. "Don't you, Jane?"

It had suddenly become very hot. Jane got up and walked with Sidney and Lillian towards the house. She hadn't planned on telling Sidney her idea, at least not right away.

"I think we should join Rachel and Matthew," she said. "My idea is not important."

Lillian laughed. "Maybe not important, but I bet it's interesting. Please tell us. It'll give us something to look forward to during the drive."

Sidney seemed to sense Jane's reluctance. "If she doesn't want to tell us yet, there's no need to."

Jane didn't know what to do. She wanted to share her idea, but she wasn't sure she had the courage to tell both Lillian and Sidney here on the lawn, in broad daylight.

"Is it something naughty?" Lillian asked.

"Of course it is," Sidney shot back. "Otherwise she wouldn't be so reluctant."

"Come on, Jane, tell us," Lillian wheedled. "What is going on in that dirty little mind of yours?"

Jane's face was on fire, but she squared her shoulders and looked at Lillian. "Tonight I want you to show me how to suck Sidney's cock."

Lillian's mouth fell open and Sidney made a strangled sound. Jane took a small measure of satisfaction from the fact she had shocked both of them. She looked over at Sidney, feeling bolder now. "Or would you not be comfortable with that?"

She let her gaze trail down to the apex of his thighs where the outline of his erect cock was visible. She smiled. "Hmm… I think I have my answer already."

She turned on her heel and walked into the house, leaving the other two on the patio. Once inside the house, she exhaled. Let them think about her proposal for a bit; no need to ask for an answer right away. Although she already knew the answer, because of what she had overheard the previous day. The butterflies in her stomach settled down, making way for a deeper pull in her lower belly. They still had the whole day to endure before they could enact her fantasy. It would be torture, but the wait would be worth it.

"Jane, wait!" Lillian hurried up to her. Jane stopped and turned to face her. "Did you mean that?" Lillian asked.

"Yes, I did."

"You're sure you want me there with Sidney?"

"I'm sure. I have no idea what I'm doing and I'd love to make him feel as good as he makes me feel. I guess you have more experience with men than I, so you could show me. Just like you helped me when Sidney fucked me the first time. Or would you rather not?" Jane plied her features into a concerned look. She realised belatedly she wasn't supposed to know that Lillian and Sidney had fucked.

"I'd love to show you," Lillian said and kissed her. "I can't wait."

"Me neither," said Sidney, coming up behind them.

Jane grinned. "It'll be a lot of fun."

Lillian put an arm around her and pulled her close. "As long as you do exactly as we say."

Jane felt a flutter of excitement in her belly. "I will."

"Good girl," Lillian said. She looked over to Sidney. "I told you she was a good little slut."

Jane couldn't stop the whimper that escaped her. She was going to melt into a puddle if they didn't stop this now.

"She's certainly a horny slut. Whether she's any good with her mouth remains to be seen." Sidney's voice was hoarse with desire and Jane's panties flooded. Why did they have to take that stupid drive?

Lillian kissed Jane's cheek and smoothed her hair. "Don't worry," she told Sidney. "I'll make sure she performs well. And if not..." she tightened her fist around a clump of Jane's hair, "...she'll be punished for it."

Jane's legs were jelly and she stumbled. Lillian grabbed her arm and grinned. "You like that, don't you?"

Jane nodded mutely.

"Damn Rachel and her plans," Sidney said. "I don't know if I can last the day."

Lillian's look could have cut glass. "You better. The higher the build-up, the greater the release. We need you in peak form tonight."

Rachel's head appeared around the door. "Are you guys coming? What's taking you so long?"

Jane grinned and skipped towards the front door. "Coming!" It was going to be a good night; she was happy she had told Lillian and Sidney her idea.

CHAPTER 19

Jane could hardly concentrate on where they were going. Her thoughts kept straying to what Lillian and Sidney had promised her. It had been her idea, but they had made it so much sexier.

Matthew was driving with Rachel beside her while Jane sat wedged in between Lillian and Sidney in the back. Their thighs pressed against her, but they otherwise did not seek out any contact with her. It killed her to sit here, her cunt throbbing but unable to alleviate the tension that was building up inside her body. She wanted to reach out and stroke Lillian's thigh, seek out her hot core, but she clamped her hands in her lap. Lillian and Sidney were in charge, and she liked it that way. She hated being told what to do by Uncle Henry, but when Sidney and Lillian ordered her around, it turned her on. She didn't even begin to understand it.

She stared out the window, her thoughts on the fun that lay ahead. Would she really be able to wait until the night? It seemed an impossibly long way off. She couldn't help grimacing – a day without sex was too long? She had really earned the title slut. Not that it bothered her; she loved it when Sidney or Lillian called her that. "Their filthy slut" – that described her well. And she was proud of it. She felt more herself as a slut than a prim, conservative prude.

She froze at that thought. Here was the answer to her troubled questions the night before. She had wondered who she was. A slut. That was how she felt most like herself. When ordered around by Lillian and Sidney, tasked to do their sexual bidding. Whether this was right or moral did not matter. It was who she was.

She focused on the landscape outside the window and suddenly sat up. It all looked familiar and with a sinking feeling she realised where they were.

"I used to live around here," she said. "I had no idea we were so close to my childhood home."

Matthew turned from the front seat. "Really? That's awesome. Do you want to find your old home? We can drive by for old times' sake."

"That would be fun," Lillian said. "I'd love to see where you grew up."

Jane hesitated. "I'd love to see my home again, but I'm not sure I can give you any directions. I've never had to make my own way there."

"I know where it is," Rachel said. "I'll direct you," she added to Matthew.

Jane's heart pounded as they got closer to her old house. She hadn't been back here since the death of her parents. Uncle Henry had sold it off to pay for her father's debts and had refused to allow her to say goodbye. Or even to get some of her personal items she had left behind. She didn't know how she would react to seeing her childhood home again.

They turned into the familiar drive and Jane gasped. Everything was the same as she remembered: the large oak trees that lined the drive, the white pillars flanking the front entrance of the house. Matthew pulled the car in front and stopped. He turned to look at Jane.

"Do you want to go in?"

"Go in?" To her surprise, Jane found that she did. "I'd love to, but how do we even know anyone is home? And we can't really knock on the door and expect these people to let us in. We're strangers to them."

"You can always try," Rachel pointed out. "The windows are open, so someone must be home."

Lillian took her hand. "Do you want me to come with you?"

Jane swallowed. "Yes, please."

They all exited the car. Lillian and Jane walked up to the front door and knocked.

A few seconds later the door opened. Jane gaped. She had not expected her parents' old butler at the door.

"Harrods, what are you doing here?"

Harrods' usual grave face cracked open into a smile. "Miss Jane," he said. "I am so happy to see you. I thought you'd never visit! I am so happy to see you well."

"What do you mean well? I haven't been sick."

Confusion reigned on Harrods's face. "Your uncle said…"

A horrid suspicion grew in Jane. "May we come in, Harrods?"

"Pardon me, miss, I should have let you in. I was stunned to see you, forgive me."

He stepped aside and Jane and Lillian entered the cool front hall. Jane gasped. Everything was still the same as when she had last been here. There was the large wardrobe where she used to hide as a child playing hide and seek with her mother. It was a monstrosity of a thing, and her father had complained more than once that it didn't belong in the hall, but her mother had loved it. Jane's eyes fell on the low table with her mother's prized vases on it. Pale pink flowers on a white background, the porcelain almost translucent. As a child she had always worried about knocking them over, but her mother had been oddly unconcerned about that. Even though the vases were her pride and joy.

Tears stung Jane's eyes at the memories. How could everything still be the same after all those years? Even the grandfather clock, which had never worked and which her mother had wanted to get rid of for years was still in its usual place at the bottom of the stairs.

Lillian slipped her hand in hers. "Are you all right?"

"Something's wrong," Jane said. "Why would Harrods think I'm sick? And why is he still here?"

"I will get your aunt," Harrods said, his voice hesitant.

Jane mustered up a smile. "That would be lovely, thank you."

Harrods disappeared and Jane pulled Lillian into the morning room. That, too, looked untouched. Even the threadbare rug with its stains where Jane had spilled her tea more than once was still on the floor.

She sat down on one of the sofas, the cushions moulding around her as if they remembered her still. She gripped Lillian's hand as if that could keep her grounded. A few minutes later they could hear rapid footsteps in the hall. Jane got up and faced the door. Aunt Lydia opened the door. She looked flustered, but tried a smile when she saw Jane.

"Jane!" she said. "What a pleasant surprise."

Anger rose in Jane like an ugly beast. "Explain," she said, her voice cold. She crossed her arms in front of her chest.

Aunt Lydia moved as if to enter the room, but Jane didn't move out of her way. Aunt Lydia took a few hesitant steps backwards. "I..." she started.

Jane almost felt sorry for her, but then she remembered how Aunt Lydia had never stood up for her against Uncle Henry and her heart hardened.

"Why are you here?" she asked. "Why is Harrods still here and why is everything still the same? Is this where you go each summer? To my house?" She spat the last words while advancing on Aunt Lydia, who skittered back into the hall.

"Your uncle…" Aunt Lydia stammered.

"Yes, I imagine it must've been his idea. That lying piece of shit."

Aunt Lydia gasped. "Jane!"

"Where is he?" Jane demanded, ignoring her. "I want to have a word with him."

Aunt Lydia mustered up some courage and drew herself up. "He's not here, and I would kindly ask you to leave."

Jane couldn't believe her ears. "I'm not leaving. In fact, I'm going to invite my friends in and we're all going to wait here until Uncle Henry returns. And then I will have a talk with him."

Whatever courage Aunt Lydia had left her and she sagged. "He should be back soon." Her voice was nothing more than a murmur.

"Great." Jane stalked away from Aunt Lydia towards the front door. Lillian hurried in her wake. Jane wrenched open the door and called out to the others, "Please come in."

She held tight to her anger, fuelling it, so that she wouldn't break down and cry. She didn't want to think of the implication of what was going on, she wanted to yell and scream at Uncle Henry.

Matthew, Rachel and Sidney entered the hall.

"Is everything okay?" Rachel asked. She looked around. "Everything looks the same."

"Everything is not okay," Jane said. "It seems that my aunt and uncle have stolen my house from me and are using it as a summer home."

"I knew something was fishy," Rachel muttered with a look at Jane's face. "I just didn't think it was this bad."

Sidney took her arm. "You didn't know this?"

"Of course I didn't," Jane spat. "Do you really think I would've allowed this to happen? This is my home. They have no right to be here."

Sidney's mouth set in a grim line. "Then we'll have to get it back for you."

Hope blossomed in Jane's heart but she ignored it. She needed to keep the anger; she'd deal with everything else later.

"Great," she told Sidney. "But first I need to yell at Uncle Henry."

He laughed, but sobered up when he saw the look on her face.

"Let's go into the living room, where we can all await my uncle's arrival," Jane said and she swept from the hall into the living room, not bothering to see if anyone followed her.

They sat down on the sofas and chairs in the living room. The atmosphere was tense and awkward, but Jane didn't care to try and lighten it. She dug her nails into her hands, relishing the pain in her palms. She hoped Uncle Henry would arrive soon; she wasn't sure how long she could last before breaking down.

CHAPTER 20

They did not have to wait long. Not long after they had sat down the front door opened and shut with a loud bang. Footsteps sounded in the hall and then Uncle Henry's voice called out.

"Lydia? Do we have visitors?"

"In here, Henry," Aunt Lydia called feebly from the living room.

Jane rose as Uncle Henry entered. He stopped in his tracks when he saw Jane.

"Hello, Uncle Henry," she said. "Take a seat."

"What are you doing here?" he asked, puffing out his chest. "Aren't you supposed to be in New York?"

"Sit. Down."

Uncle Henry blanched, but held his ground. "Don't tell me what to do in my own house, girl," he said. "And what did you do to yourself? What is that dress you are wearing and why did you cut your hair?"

"Shut up," Jane said, shaking with anger. "This is my house. You stole it from me."

"I did no such thing," Uncle Henry said. "Your parents were careless with money and the house was payment for their debt."

135

"You said you had sold it, but that was a lie," Jane said. "You took it for yourself. And I don't believe for one minute that my parents had debts."

"What do you know?" Uncle Henry's lip curled contemptuously. "You're a girl and it would behove you to leave business matters to men."

He looked around the room as if realising for the first time that they were not alone. His eye fell on Rachel and he scoffed.

"I could've known she was behind this," he spat, pointing an accusatory finger at Rachel. "You went to visit her, didn't you? I bet you've been whoring around with her, that wicked woman. I bet she cut your hair and made you wear a dress that befits a whore. I never knew why your parents allowed her to be so close to you. Even back then she was a whore and she clearly hasn't changed her ways since she got older."

Rachel arched her eyebrows, but it was Sidney who jumped up. "Don't you dare speak like that," he said.

Jane's heart warmed at seeing his indignation. Uncle Henry, however, was not cowed.

"I will speak any way I want to speak. You have no right to come into my home and tell me how to behave."

Jane could have stamped her foot with anger, but she restrained herself. "You're a liar and a thief," she said with barely concealed contempt. "And I will prove it. I will take my home back."

"Stop playing, girl," Uncle Henry sneered. "You've had your little fun, but now it's time for you to go back to New York where you can wait until I return and decide how to deal with you."

"I'll do no such thing." Heat flooded Jane's cheeks. "I'm done with you telling me what to do."

"You don't know what you're saying," Uncle Henry said. "Do you really think these whores will have your back? They aren't loyal to anyone, they're just interested in having some fun. Did they turn you to their wicked ways as well?"

Jane drew herself up to her full height. "You will not talk about my friends like that," she said.

"Friends?" Uncle Henry scoffed. "I wouldn't call them friends. People who lie with each other outside of wedlock aren't friends, they are deviants."

"Then I'm a deviant as well," Jane said. She pulled Lillian towards her. "I had sex with her." She pointed to Sidney. "And with him. In fact, I've had sex with both of them together."

Uncle Henry's face turned purple. He squinted at Lillian. "Hey, I know her. She's that sinful singer that barely wears anything on stage." He looked back at Jane. "And you…" he hesitated before spitting out, "lay with this whore?"

"Don't you dare call her that," Jane hissed. "I love Lillian and I will not have you call her names."

Uncle Henry's mouth opened and closed wordlessly. Lillian took Jane's hand in hers.

"Maybe we should go," she said quietly.

"Yes, go," Uncle Henry shouted. "And don't think you can ever return. I'll ban you from our house forever. And when your so-called friends have used you up and spat you out, don't think you can come crawling back to us. You're dead to me, hear me? Dead!"

Aunt Lydia made a strangled noise, but Jane paid her no attention. She stood rooted on the spot until Sidney put his arm around her.

"Let's go," he said.

Jane nodded reluctantly. There was no more to be gained from shouting at Uncle Henry.

"This isn't over," she said through clenched teeth. "I will get back my home."

She let Lillian and Sidney lead her out of the house. Once outside, she took a deep breath. Her legs were shaking and she felt hot all over.

"Let's get you home," Rachel suggested gently.

Matthew exhaled loudly. "I thought my parents were bad when they found out about Richard." He shook his head. "I'm so sorry your Aunt and Uncle are so narrow-minded."

The kindness of her friends nearly undid Jane. She fought back the tears that threatened to spill. Lillian and Sidney helped her into the car. They drove away in silence.

Once they were some distance away from the house, Jane exhaled shakily. "I can't believe it," she said. "I can't believe he took my home."

Suddenly the magnitude of what had happened hit her and she started crying. Lillian put her arm around her and kissed the top of her head.

"We'll sort it out," she soothed.

"I can look into the legalities, if you want," Sidney offered. "There's no way Uncle Henry would've been able to take the house as payments of your parents' debts, if they even had debts. The house would have been sold to settle them."

Jane smiled gratefully at him. "I'd really appreciate that," she said.

She felt annoyed at herself that she hadn't been able to defy Uncle Henry. At least she hadn't broken down in front of him, but she had allowed herself to be sent away without any victory. The only good thing that had resulted from the confrontation was that she was now more determined than ever to ignore Uncle Henry's words. She had felt guilty about her sexual excesses this summer, but now she saw with startling clarity that it was Uncle Henry who was in the wrong. There was nothing bad or immoral about being intimate with another person. Only Uncle Henry had made it into a sinful thing. Hearing Uncle Henry use those vile words when speaking about Rachel and Lillian made her realise how ridiculous his beliefs were. She would no longer allow his teachings to bring her down, or doubt herself.

She lay her head on Lillian's shoulder and took Sidney's hand in hers. This was where she was safe. Uncle Henry could rant and rave all he wanted, but she felt loved by these two people, and they were the only ones who deserved her love and consideration.

CHAPTER 21

The discovery of Uncle Henry's treachery put a damper on the day and they ate their lunch in a gloomy mood. After lunch, Sidney retreated to the library.

"I'll write some letters to colleagues of mine to find out more," he said. "If there's even a hint of wrongdoing, I'll go to New York and sort it out."

Rachel scoffed. "Of course there will be wrongdoing. He stole Jane's home, plain and simple."

"Jane's father may have gifted it to him in his will," Sidney pointed out.

"He'd never do that," Jane protested. "There was no love lost between father and Uncle Henry."

"In that case, we'll be able to get you your home back, but in the meantime, I'll need to find out as much as I can."

"Of course," Jane said, chastised. "I'll defer to your expertise."

Sidney kissed her and Jane melted into his arms. "I will get to the bottom of this," he said.

Jane hugged him. "Thank you so much."

Matthew had been pacing the room, but approached Sidney now. "I'll help. My legal expertise is in inheritance law, so I would like to offer my assistance. People like that shouldn't get away with their vile behaviour."

Sidney nodded. "Thank you, I appreciate that."

Jane got up and hugged Matthew. "Thank you so much. I'm sorry you had to experience something similar."

Matthew's mouth set in a grim line. "It's ridiculous that people feel the need to label us as deviants when our only crime is loving another person."

Jane couldn't agree more. She hadn't expected Uncle Henry's approval, but the fury he had poured out over her had taken her aback.

"We'll get your home back," Sidney promised.

Jane departed the library and entered the living room. The house was cool and quiet and she wanted a place to think. She lay down on the couch, her heart full of emotions.

She had been brave and defiant in the face of Uncle Henry's ire, but now that her anger had cooled, the realisation of her predicament hit her. Uncle Henry had cut her off and tossed her out. She hadn't wanted to go back to live with him and Aunt Lydia after the summer, but it had been good to know that it was at least a possibility, a safety net. Now she had nothing. No place to live, no way to support herself. It dawned on her that maybe she should not have let her emotions run away with her.

The door opened and Jane looked up to see Lillian enter. She sat on the edge of the sofa and took Jane's hand.

"How are you doing?"

Jane gave a short laugh. "I feel like I've made the biggest mistake of my life. Where am I going to live now? And what am I going to live on?"

"You'll figure something out," Lillian said vaguely. "Did you mean what you said?"

"Everything," Jane said. "If you're suggesting I go back and apologise…"

Lillian put a finger on Jane's lips. "I am not suggesting that at all. I just want to know if you meant what you said about me."

Memory flooded back and Jane sat up, startled. Had she really told Uncle Henry that she loved Lillian? Judging from Lillian's expression that was exactly what she had said. There was no backing out now. She had meant it.

"Yes," she said. "I did mean that."

"Wow," Lillian said softly. "I don't think I've ever had someone tell me that before."

Jane swallowed a lump of disappointment. She hadn't really expected Lillian to fall at her feet in love and adoration, but she would have liked a warmer response than this. She also found it hard to believe that no one had ever told Lillian that they loved her. She was a famous – and well-liked singer – and it did not seem possible that Lillian hadn't had any admirers.

She sat up and smiled. "I don't expect anything from you," she said. "And I hope this doesn't change anything between us."

Lillian kissed her. "No, of course it doesn't. I'm very lucky to have an admirer like you."

Admirer? Jane wasn't an admirer of Lillian, at least not in the way Lillian meant. But she smiled brightly and kissed her back. It was not possible to take her words back, but she would work very hard at making Lillian forget she ever said them. She didn't want things to become awkward between them, and she certainly didn't want to change the fun they had been having.

"Would you mind if I spent some time alone?" she asked Lillian.

"Of course not." Lillian got up from the sofa. "If you need me, I'll be in my room."

"Okay," Jane said, and she watched Lillian walk away, her heart heavy.

She lay back down and groaned. Everything was going wrong today. She still couldn't believe that Uncle Henry had been using her parents' house as a summer home all this time. The nerve of him! He had led her to believe that her parents had died in debt. It had always been a bit puzzling to Jane why her parents had been in debt when, during their lifetime, they had wanted for nothing, but she had only been a child when they died. Her parents wouldn't have confided in her.

Bile rose in her throat at the memory of Uncle Henry's contorted face. He had deceived her and lied about her parents. She didn't care what Sidney unearthed. She refused to believe Uncle Henry had come by her house honestly. He certainly hadn't acted like an innocent man. It shouldn't have surprised her though. For all his preaching about morality, Uncle Henry always did have a nasty streak. She just didn't think he would be this devious.

The idea of actually getting her home back, even though that was a remote possibility, excited her. It would certainly solve her problem of where to live. She would have a home of her own. But her excitement dampened when she realised she'd still need money. Harrods didn't work for free, and neither did the cook and maids and any of the other staff. She wasn't even sure how to run a household. Having a home was one, maintaining it would be a whole different story.

She groaned and turned to her side. There was no point analysing everything that had been said and done. Only time – and Sidney and Matthew' sleuthing – would tell what was going to happen to her. In the meantime, she would still have a place at Rachel's, at least for the rest of the summer. And Lillian had not seemed put out by her declaration of love, even if she didn't reciprocate, so that was also a bright spot in the day.

Jane hoped that their plans for tonight were still going ahead. She needed a diversion from her thoughts and worries. And she wanted to feel good again.

CHAPTER 22

Dinner was a livelier affair. Jane had had a nap and felt refreshed, and the others, perhaps picking up on her brighter mood, were in good spirits as well. After dinner, Matthew excused himself to go pick up Richard and Rachel withdrew to the library.

"How are you feeling?" Sidney asked. He had been in the library all afternoon writing letters and had only emerged for dinner.

"Much better," Jane said. "I guess I'll just have to wait and see what comes out of these letters."

"Exactly," Lillian agreed. "No point in worrying about things you can't control."

Jane smiled at her.

"So…" Sidney said.

"What do you want to do tonight?" Lillian asked.

Jane looked from Lillian to Sidney. "You don't have to treat me like I'm fragile," she said. "I'm fine and I was hoping we'd go ahead with my proposal."

Lillian and Sidney exchanged a glance. "Are you sure about that?" Lillian asked.

"Yes," Jane said firmly. "I need a diversion. I want to learn how to pleasure you with my mouth," she added to

Sidney.

Sidney grinned. "I'm never going to say no to that."

Lillian still seemed hesitant. Jane took her hand and pulled her towards her. "Lillian, I need this. I need to be taken care of. I want you and Sidney to use me in any way you see fit. I've been told what to do all my life by that unpleasant man, and now I want to be told what to do by the two people I care about."

Lillian nodded. "Then that's what we'll do. Let's go to my room."

Excitement coursed through Jane and she felt light-headed when she stood up. She hadn't lied: she wanted to forget today had happened and the only way she could do that was if Lillian and Sidney gave her so much pleasure she couldn't think straight.

When they got to Lillian's bedroom, Lillian took control.

"Both of you, undress," she said. "Jane, I want you kneeling on the bed, facing the edge of the bed. And Sidney, you may stand in front of Jane."

Jane shook with excitement and she fumbled with the buttons on her dress. Finally she was free and she flung her dress on the floor. Her undergarments followed. She took position on the bed just as Lillian had ordered.

Lillian had undressed as well, but had kept her stockings and shoes on. The sight of her naked sex above her stockinged legs made Jane's cunt throb with need. She wanted Lillian's gorgeous legs wrapped around her face as she licked Lillian's juices from her cunt. That would have to wait, though, as she was here to learn how to suck Sidney's cock.

Sidney approached the bed and stood in front of her. His cock was erect, pointing directly at her belly.

"On your hands and knees," Lillian commanded. "You need to be able to take him into your mouth."

Jane did as she was told and now Sidney's cock was directly in front of her face. Lillian caressed the back of her head and she almost purred with delight.

"You said you wanted us to use you," Lillian said.

Jane nodded, staring mesmerised at Sidney's cock.

"What did you mean by that?"

"I want you to fuck me," Jane said, deliberately using crude language. "Any which way. Do whatever you want to do to me."

"Anything?" Lillian asked.

Jane looked up and locked eyes with her. "Anything," she said with emphasis.

Lillian shared a glance with Sidney, who nodded. A smile crept over her face.

"Okay," she said. "But I will give you a word."

"A word?" Jane repeated, confused.

"Yes, a word you can say if you really want to stop. If you say "no" or "stop" we will carry on, but if you use that word, we will stop."

Jane's heart pounded. This sounded dangerous, but in an exciting way. "I like that. What is the word?"

"Uncle Henry," Lillian replied.

Jane burst out laughing. "Really?"

"It's a word you wouldn't think of using in this setting," Lillian explained. "So when you do use it, it's deliberate. I want you to think before you tell us to stop."

It made sense to Jane and she nodded. This evening promised to be very interesting indeed.

"Is there anything you don't want us to do?" Sidney asked.

Jane sat back on her heels to look at him. She considered his question. She was still very much a novice at sex, so she wasn't sure whether there was anything she didn't like.

"You did like being spanked, right?" Lillian asked.

Heat suffused Jane as she remembered her spankings. "Oh yes," she breathed. "I liked that very much."

"So you're not averse to a bit of pain."

Jane shook her head, her mouth dry. "I want you to

order me around," she whispered. "I don't know why, but that excites me very much. And maybe also..." she hesitated to say the words, "...restrict me," she finished.

A wicked grin spread over Lillian's face. She shared another glance with Sidney. "You mean, tie you up?" she asked. Jane could hear the lust and excitement in her voice.

She nodded. "I don't know why, but the thought appeals to me very much."

Lillian smiled. "We can certainly do that."

Jane licked her lips and looked at Sidney's cock. The tip was leaking some fluid and she wanted to lick it and taste him.

"Can I start now?" she asked.

Sidney exhaled loudly. "I thought you'd never ask," he said.

"Of course you can," Lillian said sweetly.

Jane resumed her position on her hands and knees. Lillian placed her hand on the back of Jane's head and guided her towards Sidney's cock.

"Now, open your mouth wide," she instructed.

Jane opened her mouth wide. Sidney's cock looked impossibly long and thick – how would she ever fit it into her mouth?

"Cover your teeth with your lips and relax your throat," Lillian said.

Jane felt a shiver of fear when Lillian pushed her closer to Sidney's cock. She stuck out her tongue and licked the tip. Sidney groaned and grabbed the back of her head.

"You want my cock, you filthy slut?" he growled.

The words connected with Jane's cunt and her juices seeped out of her. She whimpered and allowed him to slide his cock into her mouth. It slid in deep and hit the back of her throat, making her gag.

"Relax," Lillian said.

Jane tried and Sidney pushed himself deeper. "Stay still," he said as he pulled out slightly and then moved back inside.

Tears stung Jane's eyes as he hit the back of her throat again, but she relaxed and he slid down deeper.

"Now close your lips around his cock," Lillian said.

Jane did so and Sidney moaned. It was hard to swallow, and soon Jane's chin and throat were slick with her saliva. It didn't matter to her; what mattered was that Sidney loved it. Lillian disappeared from view, but Jane paid her no attention. She focused on Sidney, his hand on the back of her head pushing her towards his cock at each thrust. His movements became rougher as his pleasure heightened and Jane smiled to herself. She was happy she had decided to learn this particular way of pleasing Sidney; his groans fanned the flames of her own lust. She wanted to make him come; receive his seed in her mouth and lick him clean.

Then Lillian's voice sounded behind her. "You like sucking cock? You're filthy, aren't you? I think you need to be spanked."

Jane would have cried out "yes" if she could; instead she moaned around Sidney's cock. Lillian evidently took that as agreement, as a hard slap landed on Jane's ass, propelling her forward on Sidney's cock.

She moaned with delight when Lillian's hand stroked her sore ass, only to slap her again. She closed her eyes and allowed herself to be suspended in sensation: Sidney's thrusts in her mouth and Lillian's hand on her ass.

Sidney's breathing became rapid, his moans louder. Jane couldn't help feeling a surge of pride with each moan she elicited from him. Lillian's caressed her ass in between her slaps, creeping closer to her sex after each one. Her cunt ached with the need to be touched and when, after another hard slap, Lillian's fingers slid through her slit, it took all her willpower not to cry out in delight. She pushed her hips back as far as she could and Lillian got the message. She stopped spanking Jane; instead, she slipped two fingers into her cunt and started thrusting at the same speed as Sidney.

The pleasure was almost too much for Jane, but she returned her focus to Sidney. She struggled to stay upright, as Lillian's fingers made her shake with pleasure, but she was determined to bring Sidney to an orgasm. She wanted to know what it was like to receive his seed into her mouth. Sidney's thrusts slowed down, but his cock grew rock hard in her mouth. He grabbed the hair at the back of her head and held her in place. He emitted a low moan and stilled. She felt something hot spurt out and hit the back of her throat as he climaxed in her mouth; gagging, she swallowed. Lillian withdrew her fingers despite the fact that Jane had not reached her climax yet.

"You better not waste a drop," Sidney growled, holding her head still until she had sucked and licked him clean. The words made her moan with desire. When she had licked every drop, he released her and kissed her briefly. "Well done, that was really good."

Jane couldn't help the whimper that escaped her. His words filled her with wild need. Her nipples were painfully erect and her clit begged to be stroked. She wasn't sure how long she could stand not being able to orgasm.

"My turn," Lillian said. "I want to have some fun as well."

Jane was hot with lust and she looked up at Lillian with pleading eyes.

"I think it's time to tie her up," Lillian observed.

Jane gasped. She had not expected Lillian to tie her up so soon in the proceedings, but her excitement outweighed her fear.

"On your back, arms behind your head and your legs spread." Lillian's voice was rough and commanding.

Jane lay down, every cell in her body buzzing with arousal. A sheen of sweat covered her body and she felt dizzy.

Lillian rummaged in her bedside table and emerged with a few long, thin scarves. She held them up to Sidney. "We can use these."

Sidney nodded. He took two scarves from Lillian and the two of them tied Jane up.

"That's not too tight?" Sidney asked, a look of concern on his face.

Jane scowled at him. He was ruining the moment. She didn't need concern, she needed a good fucking.

"It's fine."

Lillian reached over a tweaked one of Jane's nipples hard. Jane squealed with pain and whipped her head around to look at Lillian.

Lillian smiled at her. "That's for scowling," she said. "You're altogether too naughty for your own good."

"I'm so sorry," Jane demurred and she could tell from the flush on Lillian's face that it had been the right response.

Jane was completely exposed. Her knees were bent and tied up to her thighs and to the bed, putting her on full display with no way to escape. Her juices trickled out of her onto the bed and her cunt was hot with need. She badly wanted to ask for pleasure, but she refrained. She didn't want another punishment; at least not yet.

Lillian knelt between Jane's legs and fastened her mouth to her sex, sending a shock of pleasure through Jane's body. Lillian licked her slit, making appreciative noises as she did so.

"So wet," she said, looking up at Jane. "Such a horny, filthy cunt."

Jane thought she wouldn't be able to stand it much longer: each word drove her wild with desire.

Sidney joined Lillian and ran his fingers through her slit. "Wet and ready, don't you think?" he asked Lillian.

Jane loved how they spoke about her as if she wasn't there. She was gasping for relief – something, anything! – and almost whimpered when Lillian moved away. Sidney took her place and plunged two fingers inside her gaping hole. Jane moaned, but he withdrew them just as quickly.

"Please," Jane whispered. "Please fuck me already."

"I love hearing you beg," Lillian purred.

She trailed her fingers over Jane's folds again. Her touch was feather light, and Jane thought she would shatter in a million pieces if she didn't get a proper fucking. She considered using her special word. She didn't want Lillian to tease her any longer, but she held her tongue. She willed herself to take a deep breath and relax. Her cunt ached, painfully now, but she trusted that Lillian would reward her well for her patience.

Lillian's fingers fluttered over Jane's clit and she whimpered. "Please…"

"Enough teasing," Sidney said. "I think she deserves a proper fucking."

Lillian smiled at Jane. "Such a good, patient girl. Let's start."

She grabbed one of her dildos and held it up for Jane to see. Jane's eyes widened at the sight of it. It was big with a bulbous tip and it looked made of stone. It looked like it would be a challenge to fit, and for a moment she quailed. But then desire overtook her fear. She wanted to be challenged, even if it was going to hurt.

"Attend to her nipples and clit, and I'll amuse myself with her cunt," Lillian told Sidney.

He grinned and shifted position so he could reach Jane better. He roughly ran his hands along Jane's body, teasing her nipples and clit until she whimpered. Then he dipped a finger into her wet core and drew out some of her juices. He spread them around her cunt and pressed down hard on her clit. Jane gasped at the sudden jolt of pleasure and arched her back in an attempt to get more of his fingers. The ropes held her in place though and she had to wait patiently for his fingers to connect with her clit again.

"Relax," he told her. "You'll get an orgasm when Lillian and I think you're ready."

Being at the mercy of the two people she loved was liberating. All she needed to do was submit herself to them. She relaxed and allowed her body to take what

Lillian and Sidney decided to give her, without straining for more.

Lillian rubbed the dildo through Jane's wet slit and she gasped. It was cold – far colder than she expected and the change in temperature shocked her. Sensations overwhelmed her: Sidney's fingers on her nipples and clit and Lillian who thrust the dildo deep inside her. She relished the cold in her aching cunt; the relief was instant.

"Let's see how much we can make her come." Lillian smiled at Jane. "We have the whole night, I want to reduce her to a sopping mess."

Sidney grinned. "That sounds wonderful."

It did sound wonderful. Jane closed her eyes and let the tension mount as wave after wave of pleasure crashed over her. Lillian was not gentle: she thrust the dildo hard in Jane's cunt, pulled it out almost all the way and thrust it back in, ramming the barrier deep inside her. Soon Jane could feel herself approaching the edge and Lillian pushed her over without hesitation. Jane cried out as the combined pleasure of her nipples, clit and cunt coursed through her body.

Lillian removed the dildo and looked over at Sidney.

"Your turn," she said.

In a daze Jane watched Sidney get up. His cock was erect again, and bigger than before. He took up position between her knees and untied the scarves. Jane wanted to protest, but when he stretched out her legs, she sighed with relief. They were sore from having been held in the same position for such a long time and she was grateful that he was looking out for her.

"Turn around, on your hands and knees," he commanded her.

She struggled to turn around, her body not completely under her command. Sidney helped her into position.

Lillian handed her a dildo. "You can fuck me while he takes care of you," she said.

Before Jane could say anything, Sidney grabbed her

hips and pulled her towards him. He spread her legs wider and placed his cock at the entrance of her cunt. Jane thought she would have been sated from Lillian's work with the dildo, but the feeling of his hot cock at her entrance reignited her lust. She pressed against him. He slid in easily and she sighed. Such a marked contrast to the cold, hard dildo.

Lillian took place in front of her and spread her legs.

"Don't waste time," she said harshly and Jane turned her attention to her.

It was hard to concentrate on pleasuring Lillian while Jane was being rammed by Sidney's cock. Her orgasm built quickly, but Lillian's pleasure was more important to her. Sidney reached around and his fingers connected with her clit. She cried out from the sheer exquisite feeling this caused. Her orgasm threatened to drown her, but Lillian reached out and pinched her nipple hard.

Jane shrieked and turned her attention back to Lillian.

"Focus on what you're doing," Lillian said. "You're not the only one wanting a climax."

Jane bent over and licked Lillian's clit as she continued to pound her with the dildo. Sidney's thrusts pushed her towards Lillian and her cunt spasmed and contracted with her prolonged orgasm. She wasn't sure how much more she could endure, but Sidney did not stop. Jane forced her focus on Lillian, who was moaning and thrashing on the bed. Jane felt like she was liquid, her body was numb with pleasure as wave after wave continued to crash over her.

And then was Sidney climaxing. He gripped her hips hard and kept her in place as his cock twitched deep inside her. Jane was barely aware of what she was doing to Lillian anymore. Sidney withdrew and cupped Jane's cunt with his hand, running lazy circles over her clit. She moaned, and it took all her effort to focus on Lillian. During her orgasm she had lifted her head and Lillian's fingers were now furiously rubbing her own clit.

Jane thought she would pass out from the pleasure, and

considered using her word. But she wanted to endure, she wanted to show Lillian and Sidney that she could keep up with them. So, in spite of her shaking legs and ragged breath, she thrust the dildo back into Lillian's cunt and didn't stop until Lillian came shuddering on the dildo and grabbed her hand to stop her.

"Oh fuck, that's good," Lillian moaned.

Jane thought Sidney would stop now that Lillian was satisfied, but he kept his fingers on her clit, drawing out one more orgasm from her ravaged body. She moaned and fell forward onto the bed, pinning Sidney's hand underneath her. He pushed forward and slid a finger inside her, while maintaining his other fingers on her clit. Jane reached down grabbed his hand.

"Uncle Henry," she rasped, feeling silly for saying it, but unable to endure any more pleasure.

Sidney withdrew his hand and stretched out beside her. "Good girl, you remembered the word." He kissed her neck.

Heat flushed Jane's face. She panted heavily and it took a while for her to get her breath under control.

"I had a lot of fun," she said at last.

Lillian lay down and pulled Jane into a tight embrace. "I'm glad you had fun. You did so well. I never expected you to endure that much."

Jane grinned, feeling immensely proud. "Well, I am a slut, remember?"

"And what a delicious slut," Sidney said.

Lillian kissed her. "It's great how you trusted us."

"Of course," Jane replied. "I know you were only concerned with my pleasure."

"Well…" Lillian said. "Not only your pleasure."

Jane laughed and snuggled closer between Sidney and Lillian. She felt safe, sated beyond belief and grateful for two such great lovers.

CHAPTER 23

Jane tried to put Uncle Henry's treachery out of her mind over the next couple of days. Sidney didn't expect and answer to his enquiry within the week, so there was nothing anyone could do but wait. Matthew had excused himself to spend some time with Richard, promising he would assist Sidney as soon as Sidney had received news from his contacts in the city.

Lillian and Sidney tried hard to keep Jane distracted, and were mostly successful. After their wonderful night, they had not spent any further time together, much to Jane's disappointment. She had spent time with Lillian and Sidney separately, but never together and Jane started to wonder why. Was it simply because she never suggested it again? It couldn't be because Lillian and Sidney didn't like being together – their tryst by the river told a different story.

She went for a walk by the side of the river to clear her head. A thunderstorm the night before had cleared the air and the breeze was pleasantly cool. Jane could get used to this life. Long walks by the river, good sex at night. Nothing to worry her little head over. She scoffed at herself. Dreaming wouldn't do her any good.

"So, what are you going to do if you find out you are rich?"

Jane looked over and saw Lillian by her side. She has been so lost in thought she hadn't heard her arrive.

"I'm going to live a life of luxury," she joked. "Like Rachel."

Lillian threaded her arm through Jane's. "That sounds lovely."

"You could join me," Jane said, getting caught up in the fantasy. "We could have late breakfasts, swim in the river, attend Rachel's parties and exhaust each other every night with satisfaction."

Lillian laughed. "I have my career."

Jane's good mood dampened slightly. "True." She thought quickly. "Then you could sing during the evening and return home to me. I'd feed you, massage you and then pleasure you."

"It's a nice fantasy," Lillian said. "Sadly we live in the reality."

Jane's heart sank. "Yes, we do."

"But the reality might be that you are a rich woman, so don't lose heart. You may yet have your life of luxury."

A life of luxury without Lillian in it didn't sound so appealing to Jane, but she didn't say anything. She didn't want to ask Lillian whether there was a place in her life for Jane after the summer. She didn't want to be rejected. The summer was rapidly coming to an end and Jane couldn't bear the thought of parting.

"And Sidney?" Lillian asked. "How does he feature in this fantasy of yours?"

"Oh, he's there too," Jane said lightly. "I've been having too much fun with the both of you to leave him out."

They crossed the lawn towards the house. Sidney stood on the patio, a frown on his face. Jane's heart sank. A frowning Sidney could only mean bad news.

Sidney's face cleared when he saw them. "Having fun

without me again?"

Jane grinned at him. "Not willingly. In fact, I've been wondering if you've been avoiding us."

They sat down on a bench on the patio, Jane between Lillian and Sidney.

"I haven't been avoiding you," Sidney said. "I thought you could use some space."

Lillian put her hand on Jane's thigh. "When we were last together, everything was a bit overwhelming for you. We thought we'd give you some space."

A surge of irritation flashed through Jane. "I'm not a child. I loved having sex with both of you together. It wasn't overwhelming at all."

Lillian raised an eyebrow and Jane relented. "Fine, it was maybe a bit crazy, but in a good way. Besides, you could've asked me what I wanted."

"I'm sorry," Sidney said. "We only did what we thought was best for you."

Jane huffed. "And I don't get a say in it?"

"We didn't want to put any pressure on you," Lillian said. "I was worried that if we asked you, you'd feel pressured to say that you wanted threesomes all the time."

Jane opened her mouth to protest, but then thought better of it. Lillian was right: she would have been tempted to repeat that fantastic night with Lillian and Sidney over and over. But that may not have been wise. It had been too intense to repeat too often.

"I still would've liked to be consulted at least," she grumbled.

Sidney kissed her. "You're right, we should've asked you."

Jane sighed. She had been worried that that spectacular night would not be repeated. It had been intense, but she wanted to feel some of that heady rush of orgasms again. To be used, maybe even humiliated. She didn't want to think about why she felt this way. Sex with Lillian and Sidney separately kept her sated enough, but there was a wild beast inside her that had woken up. She didn't want to give it free reign all the time, but now it had awoken, she could not tame it.

"So you two liked that night as well?" she asked.

"Liked it?" Lillian said. "I loved it. And don't worry, baby, we'll definitely do something like that again."

Sidney chuckled. "We know you're almost insatiable. Another opportunity will surely present itself and we'd love to play with you like that again."

Jane rested her head on Sidney's shoulder. "I'd like that very much."

They sat in silence for a while.

"I think it's almost lunch," Lillian said. "Let's go in."

Jane reluctantly got up and followed Lillian into the house.

At lunch, Rachel announced that there was going to be another party that night. Jane was beyond excited to hear this, the timing could not have been better. She had much more experience and this was a perfect opportunity to get both her lovers together. There was something she wanted to try and she hoped both Lillian and Sidney would agree to help her.

After dinner, she rushed to get ready for the party. When she came downstairs, Rachel was overseeing the finishing touches on the preparations, but Lillian and Sidney had not arrived yet. Jane snuck a glass of champagne and retreated to the hall where she could await her lovers.

Rachel joined her. "Looking forward to tonight?"

Jane grinned. "Yes, I am. What about you? Will your mystery lover be here?"

Rachel laughed. "No, she has moved on. But that means I'm free to participate tonight."

"That will be fun." Jane took a sip of champagne and studied Rachel. She didn't seem upset that her lover had moved on, whatever that meant. Maybe it had just been a fling for Rachel. It was interesting to note that her lover had been a woman.

"Yes," Rachel mused. "I've rather neglected the guests at my parties. Tonight will be different." She turned to Jane. "And what about you? Will you participate again?"

"I'm planning to do so, yes."

Rachel put her hand on Jane's arm. "Don't get too carried away though, all right? Take care that you don't do something you regret."

"I won't."

Rachel excused herself to go and greet some guests, leaving Jane alone again.

Minutes later, Sidney descended the stairs and Jane crossed the hall to meet him.

"Excited for the party?" Sidney asked when he saw her.

"Very much so," Jane confirmed. "It's going to be fun."

Sidney grinned. "Yes, it will." He grabbed a glass of champagne. "I may even participate tonight."

Jane's heart leaped. What she had in mind for tonight would require Sidney's participation, so she was relieved to hear he intended to join in.

Lillian descended the stairs and joined them. "Did I hear that right?" she asked. "Is Sidney going to play tonight?"

Sidney turned to her. "Yes, I can't let my favourite women have all the fun alone, can I?"

Jane smiled broadly. "Perfect."

Lillian put her arm around Jane's waist. "I recognise that look. You have something in mind."

Jane swallowed, suddenly afraid her idea would be too daring. "I do," she said. "But you can't judge me."

"We'd never judge you," Lillian said. "Trust me, we love your ideas."

Sidney took her hand and kissed it. "I'm willing to do whatever makes you happy."

Jane's heart swelled two sizes at the love on his face. She took a deep breath. "I want to know what it's like to have sex with someone else. Other than you two," she added.

Sidney and Lillian shared a glance. "That shouldn't be a problem," Lillian said.

"And maybe more than just one person," Jane said, her heart pounding.

Lillian grinned. "How many people? Men, or also women?"

As always, she had seen right through Jane.

"I don't know how many," Jane confessed. "More than two."

She hardly dared look at Sidney.

His soft laugh surprised her. "Told you she was a little slut."

Jane breathed a sigh of relief. He was not angry, or jealous or judgemental. She looked up to see him grin. "This could be fun," he said.

Lillian pulled them both towards the corner of the hall. "How do you want to do this?" she asked Jane.

Now that both of them were enthusiastic about the idea, Jane could relax. "I'm not sure. You two have attended more of these parties than me, so you know more people. Maybe you can select them and organise everything?"

Sidney put his hand on her back. "We can do that."

"Do you want it to be public?" Lillian asked.

Jane clasped her hands behind her back. She took a deep breath. "Yes, I would."

"Hmmm," Sidney said, kissing her neck. "Public humiliation, sounds perfect."

"We'll look after you," Lillian promised. "This is going to be good."

Jane's cunt throbbed with lust. This was going to be her biggest night ever. To be humiliated in front of the whole room, to be fucked by strangers...she could hardly breathe from the desire that flooded her. And to know that she was in good hands, that both her lovers would look out for her, made everything perfect.

CHAPTER 24

Lillian told Jane to stay in the hall until everything was ready for her. She was not allowed to talk to anyone or participate in any sexual activities. Not that Jane wanted to – the wait heightened her arousal and she needed to be at her neediest by the time she was called. She had no idea how many men and women Lillian and Sidney would recruit for their little show, but she trusted that Lillian knew how much she could take. And if she really wanted to stop, she always had her special word. She assumed she could still use it tonight.

Finally Lillian appeared by her side. She took Jane's hand. "We're ready for you."

Jane was shaking as she followed Lillian, partly from excitement and partly from fear of what was going to happen. The fear made her arousal all the more delicious and her cunt was dripping by the time she entered the room. Lillian led her through the crowd who had evidently been told what to expect: all eyes were on her as she walked to the front of the room. A sofa had been placed facing the room; most of the attendees were gathered around it. Jane spotted Rachel towards the back of the room engaged with a man. They seemed engrossed in each other and Jane was relieved Rachel wouldn't be part of the audience.

"You're sure you want to go through with this?" Lillian whispered.

"Yes," Jane said, her voice hoarse. "I'm sure. Can I still use my special word if I need it?"

Lillian squeezed her hand. "Absolutely."

Lillian turned towards the audience. She lay a hand on Jane's shoulder and addressed the room. "This slut here wants to be fucked. By as many men and women as she can take." She moved to stand behind Jane and seized her robe. With a flourish she pulled it off Jane. "She's wet and wanting, so I don't want to waste any time. Sidney will get her started."

Jane sighed with relief. While she still wanted to go ahead with her plan, it was comforting to start off with someone familiar.

"Sit down and spread your legs," Lillian commanded her.

She did as she was told. Several people craned their necks to see her. Lillian knelt between her legs and gave her cunt a few licks, flicking her clit with the tip of her tongue. A moan escaped her and she let herself relax.

Lillian stood up and was replaced by Sidney. He smiled at her as he grabbed her hips and pulled her closer. His cock pressed against the entrance of her cunt and she bucked her hips against him.

"Nice and eager," Lillian commented, sitting down next to Jane and reaching for her clit. "Remember, ladies and gentlemen, this cunt can be yours."

Jane looked around the room, at all the faces full of lust and desire, and she smiled. This was exactly what she wanted.

Without warning Sidney rammed himself inside her and she gasped at the sudden intrusion. He took her rough, thrusting hard, pressing her into the sofa. Her cunt contracted around his cock, small shocks of pleasure

THE INSATIABLE JANE TRAVERS

shooting through her. Before she could properly start enjoying herself, he withdrew.

"Get up," he said, his voice harsh.

She shivered with lust and got shakily to her feet. He led her around to the side of the sofa and bent her over it. Lillian got up from the sofa and walked around the crowd.

Sidney stroked Jane's hair as a man took place behind her, his rough hands grabbing her hips. She gasped as she felt his cock at her entrance, but before she could fully process what was happening, he penetrated her.

Two women took place on the sofa, each taking one of her breasts into their hands. Then she felt another pair of hands on her exposed cunt, caressing her labia and strumming her clit. She hadn't realised this was what Lillian and Sidney had had in mind, but it was exactly what she needed. Lust swept through her and she bucked her hips against the cock deep inside her. The man was rough – rougher than Sidney had been, but she didn't care. She wanted it like this. It wasn't a night for tenderness, it was a night for wild fucking.

She closed her eyes, letting pleasure wash over her. Her orgasm built slowly, slower than she would have expected and it momentarily frustrated her. Everything felt amazing, her whole body being caressed and pinched and licked and pulled. She was a plaything, a doll to be fucked and stuffed. She was exactly where she wanted to be and yet an orgasm eluded her.

She moaned as she felt the man inside her stiffen and his hot seed spill deep inside her. He pulled out and she whimpered. She hadn't even come close to reaching her climax. But she needn't have worried. Someone pulled her back and a mouth fastened itself onto her cunt, sucking and licking. She didn't know who it was, didn't even know whether it was a man or a woman, but that didn't matter. Their tongue probed deep inside her cunt, fingers rubbed over her clit and she was swept up to impossible heights. She moaned and ground against this person's face, desperate to reach her climax. The two women in front of her sat up and began suckling her nipples. Her orgasm started slowly, deep inside her, sweeping her up in a tidal wave of pleasure and she bucked and moaned and cried with the sheer force of it. Her legs shook and she clung to the women in front of her while she crested the wave and fell over the edge.

Hands helped her lie down on the sofa and Lillian's face swam into focus.

"Do you want to stop?" she asked.

Jane shook her head. "More," she panted. She wanted more cocks inside her, more mouths sucking the men's come from her swollen cunt.

Lillian smiled and nodded. She straightened up. "You heard her, let's give her more," she announced.

She slipped behind Jane on the sofa and cradled her in her lap. Sidney chose the next person who was allowed to fuck her while Lillian stroked her breasts and kissed her neck. A man knelt between her legs, his cock large and stiff between his thighs. Lillian reached between Jane's thighs and spread her pussy lips open. She rubbed her clit while the man entered her.

Jane gasped as her next climax started to build. There was a tug deep in her belly that connected with her cunt, radiating waves of pleasure throughout her body. The man fucked her hard and quick, coming within minutes of entering her, but it didn't matter. He was replaced by a woman, whose expert tongue pushed Jane crashing over the edge again. She clung to Lillian as another man entered her, replaced by another woman when he had shot his load inside her.

Time lost all meaning and Jane couldn't tell where one orgasm ended and another one began. She felt weightless, suspended in a cloud of pleasure, her cunt contracting, her clit throbbing, her voice hoarse from moaning. Hands caressed her, tongues licked her and she became aware that only the women remained. They kissed her thighs and cunt and breasts; feather light kisses that softened the intensity of her orgasms until she was no more than a quivering mess on the sofa.

And then Sidney was there, wrapping a blanket around her and lifting her up. She buried her head against his chest while he carried her out of the room, up the stairs into her bedroom. He lay her down on the bed. Lillian settled herself between her thighs and began cleaning her. The cool water soothed her swollen cunt and Lillian's expert fingers worked ointment onto her sore folds. Little by little her vision cleared and she smiled at Lillian and Sidney.

"You did so well," Lillian whispered. "I'm so proud of you."

Jane stretched her hand out to her. "Thank you both for making this possible," she said.

Sidney sat next to her and stroked her head. "How are you feeling?"

"Wonderful," Jane replied. "It was intense and amazing, and I loved every minute of it."

Maybe it was the fact that she was more experienced in sex now, but she felt less overwhelmed than when she had been humiliated by Laura. Then she had felt out of it, tired beyond belief, but now she felt invigorated and alert. She sat up and embraced Lillian, kissing her deeply. Then she looked up at Sidney.

"You two haven't had any fun yet," she said. "Let's go back to the party."

Lillian laughed and pushed her back down. "You need to sleep," she said.

"But I'm not tired," Jane protested. "And I can tell Sidney hasn't been properly satisfied."

Lillian looked around at Sidney's erect cock. Sidney grimaced, but it was impossible for him to deny it.

"How can you not be tired after all that?" Lillian asked Jane incredulously.

Jane shrugged. "All those orgasms relaxed me, but I feel very much awake. And I don't want to deny you two the pleasure you deserve for taking such good care of me."

Lillian's nipples were hard peaks and she stole another glance at Sidney. Jane patted the space next to her on the bed.

"Here, lie down," she said. "If you two don't want to go to the party, then you can at least satisfy each other here."

Her own swollen, abused cunt could not endure any more pleasure, but she wanted her friends to feel at least some of the relief she was feeling.

Sidney shook his head. "You've had enough sex for the night."

"I wouldn't participate," Jane protested.

"Sidney is right," Lillian said. "We'll leave you alone."

Jane frowned, but she knew deep down that they were right. She would have loved to watch Sidney and Lillian have sex right next to her, but it was likely that it would arouse her again, and the thought of another orgasm exhausted her.

"Okay, fine," she said. "But promise me you two will have sex."

"We will," Sidney said, kissing her. "We'll see you in the morning."

Lillian kissed her as well and tucked the sheets in around her. "Good night."

"Good night," Jane said reluctantly.

When they had departed, she pulled her covers off again. It was hot in the room and her body still felt on fire from all the pleasure she had had. Her fingers gingerly touched her cunt and she gasped at how swollen everything felt. She did not regret how the evening had gone.

CHAPTER 25

Jane hadn't seen Sidney after breakfast. He had disappeared into the library to "study up on her case", hoping for news from New York soon. It had been more than a week since he had sent his letters to New York and Jane was getting anxious. What if the lack of news meant that she had no claim on the house? Or that only the house had remained and she was penniless? She tried not to worry about it too much, but it was hard to contain her impatience.

Lillian was playing tennis with Rachel, but Jane had declared it too hot to watch and had retreated to her spot on the hammock. She wanted to be alone with her thoughts. She wished news from New York would hurry up. She wanted to know what her future held. The last weeks had been amazing; spending time with Sidney and Lillian had made her realise how much she would miss them after the summer. After the sex party, Sidney and Lillian had spent more time together with Jane and she loved being taken care of by both of them. Sex was so much better with three people.

She could also no longer deny her feelings for them, but for Lillian in particular. She loved waking up next to her, playing lazily in the early morning hours, or engaging in wild, passionate sex with her and Sidney before going to sleep. It wasn't just the sex, though, she and Lillian had become friends. She couldn't imagine her life without Lillian. And Sidney? Jane's heart ached thinking about having to say goodbye to him. They had grown so close over the past few weeks, she couldn't bear to part with him again.

She sighed. If only she knew about her money, then she could plan her future. She could not make any decisions until then, and time was running out. There were only a few more weeks of summer remaining.

Lillian appeared around the corner and dropped her tennis racket next to the hammock. She slipped into the hammock next to Jane and kissed her.

"How was your game?" Jane asked.

"Good. Too hot though."

"It's too hot to have you with me in the hammock," Jane said, sliding out. "I'll sit in the grass, you deserve to rest."

Lillian didn't protest, but stretched out. "Thanks. How are you feeling?"

"Great," Jane said. "Nervous. I want Sidney to tell me how things are."

"There must be news soon," Lillian said.

"I don't want to get my hopes up," Jane said. "But if the house is mine, it'll solve so many problems."

Lillian patted Jane's head. "I'm sure it will all work out."

Rachel joined them on the lawn. "There's lemonade on the terrace," she said. "Do you gals want any?"

Lemonade sounded delicious, and Jane jumped up. She hadn't realised how parched she was until Rachel mentioned a drink.

Lillian waved them away. "I need to rest a bit more," she said. "I don't think my legs can carry me."

"Do you want me to bring you a glass?" Jane asked.

"No, thanks," Lillian said. "I just need rest."

Jane hesitated for a moment. She wanted to be with Lillian, but at the same time refreshments sounded too good to pass up. Thirst won out.

"I'll be back in a bit," she said.

The lemonade was cold and tart and what was more, Sidney came out to join them. Jane gratefully drank the refreshing liquid. She wanted to ask Sidney about her case, but he looked tired and hot, so she refrained from saying anything. He sank down in a chair and grabbed a glass of lemonade.

"Have you received any news?" Rachel asked when he finished drinking.

Jane sat on the tip of her chair.

Sidney nodded. "Yes, a letter finally arrived this morning."

Jane gasped and clasped her hands to her mouth. This was the moment of truth.

"It turns out that there was a will," Sidney said, "and you father gifted everything to you, Jane."

Jane's heart leaped. She had been right, her parents hadn't been poor after all.

"I still need to look into the details, but from what I gather, the house is yours. The house, and a whole lot of investments as well. You're a rich woman."

Rich! Jane could hardly believe it. "How rich exactly?" she asked, trying to keep her voice steady.

"Rich enough that you won't have to worry about money or getting a job for the rest of your life."

Rachel hugged her. "I'm so happy for you, Jane."

Jane was stunned. She didn't know what to feel. She was angry at Uncle Henry for trying to steal her inheritance from her, but at the same time she was overjoyed that all her problems had been solved. This meant that she wouldn't have to worry about where she would go after the summer. She had her own home and her own income!

She leaped up and kissed Sidney. "Thank you so much

for helping me with this," she said. "I can't believe Uncle Henry tried to steal it all from me."

"It will take a few weeks to get you access to all your money," Sidney warned. "Your uncle hasn't been able to touch your investments, only the house, which he tried to sell a few years ago. I'll have to go up to the city and sort it all out, but they are only formalities. You can kick your aunt and uncle out of the house now if you wanted."

Jane remembered her aunt's drawn face and shook her head. It wasn't worth breaking all bonds between her and her aunt. Besides, she had planned on staying with Rachel for the remainder of the summer. There was no reason to leave earlier.

"No, I'll wait until everything is set. Let them enjoy their last summer in my home. I will move in once everything is final."

"We'll live so close to each other," Rachel enthused. "I'm so happy!"

Jane grinned. A huge burden had been lifted from her shoulders. She hugged Rachel.

"Thank you so much for allowing me to stay here. If it hadn't been for me visiting you, I would've never found out about all of this."

"You're very welcome," Rachel said. "I'm so happy you accepted my invitation." She got up and kissed Jane. "If you'll excuse me, I need to see Cook about dinner."

She walked in the direction of the house.

Jane beamed. She felt elated. Sidney, on the other hand, looked sombre.

"What's wrong?" Jane asked him. "Are you not happy for me?"

"Of course I'm happy for you," Sidney said. "I'm preoccupied trying to think of everything that needs to be done. And I hate having to go to the city in the middle of summer. I don't like missing out, and the city will be hot and stifling at this time of the year."

Jane's heart sank. "I'm so sorry," she said. "How long

will you have to be there for?"

"Hopefully only a few days," Sidney said. "With Matthew's help, I'll be able to finish everything a lot quicker."

"I'll miss you," she said softly.

Sidney smiled wanly and Jane frowned. She felt like something had shifted between them.

She grabbed his hand and kissed it. "I'm very grateful for everything you've done for me," she said with emphasis.

"It's absolutely my pleasure," Sidney said with a bit of his old exuberance returning. He got up and dropped her hand. "I'll leave this evening, so I can start early tomorrow morning. I hope to be back in a few days."

"Thank you so much for doing this," Jane said. "And thank Matthew for me as well when you meet up with him."

Sidney nodded. "No problem." He turned and walked away.

Jane stared at his retreating back. What had got into Sidney? He hadn't even kissed her goodbye. She sighed, her elation of earlier disappearing. She poured herself another glass of the cold lemonade and looked up when she heard footsteps on the terrace. Lillian had come to join her.

"Did I just miss Sidney?" she asked.

"You did. He received a letter telling him that I do have an inheritance. I have a house and investments; enough money to live on." She still felt stunned at this.

Lillian grabbed her hands and kissed her. "That's such wonderful news, I'm so happy for you! Now you don't have to worry about where to live anymore."

"It is amazing," Jane agreed. How could she not agree? She was finally free. "I don't have to put up with my aunt and uncle anymore. I can be independent."

Lillian's hand rested on Jane's thigh and that small gesture almost brought tears to her eyes.

"Lillian -," she started, but then her nerves failed her. She wanted to tell Lillian that she loved her and that she wanted to spend her life together with her. She hadn't wanted to press the issue earlier, but that was before she knew she had money. When she had blurted out to Uncle Henry that she loved Lillian she hadn't really expected Lillian to take her seriously. Even when Lillian pressed the issue and expressed gratitude for her admiration, she hadn't wanted to correct her. Not having money or even a place to live had made her cautious. She hadn't wanted Lillian to think she was after her money.

But now things were different. She had a house and independent means; she wouldn't need Lillian's money. She didn't quite feel equal to Lillian, but her status had certainly improved.

Lillian looked at her expectantly, but Jane was too scared to continue. What if Lillian really didn't like her that way? What if she was just some fun for Lillian, to be discarded after the summer?

"Sidney seemed a bit upset," she said instead.

Lillian looked taken aback and Jane wondered if she had expected her to declare her love. She shook off the thought.

"Yes, I imagine he would be upset," Lillian said casually.

"Why though? I don't know what I've done wrong."

Lillian moved her hand higher on Jane's thigh and gave her a little squeeze. "It's nothing you've done. Sidney has been thinking about asking you to marry him, but now he realises he can't."

"Why?" Jane demanded. "Is it because we all slept together? Is it because I slept with you?"

"No, of course not." Lillian laughed. "It's because you have money now."

Jane gaped at her. The possibility had not even occurred to her. "Why would that make a difference? It would only make life easier."

"Yes, but Sidney is an old-fashioned man. He wants to be the provider in the family. He doesn't want to feel like he is kept by his wife."

"That's ridiculous," Jane protested. "What does it matter where the money comes from? And he can't be that old-fashioned if he likes having sex with two women at the same time."

Lillian grinned. "I've stopped trying to understand men. Maybe for Sidney sex is different."

Jane scoffed. "So what? He suddenly doesn't find me desirable now that I have money? That makes no sense."

"Of course he still finds you desirable, he just doesn't want to be seen as a gold digger."

Jane was irritated. Why would Sidney care what people thought of him? If he loved her – which he must if he had considered asking her to marry him – then he shouldn't care whether people thought he married her for money or not. All that should matter was their love.

"He's an idiot," Jane declared. "Well, he can suit himself. If he doesn't want to marry me, fine. I'm not going chasing after him."

Although her words were brave, her heart quailed thinking about losing Sidney. She liked him, a lot, and had done so since childhood. She had grown to love him in the time she'd spent with him at Rachel's and she didn't want to lose him again.

"He is an idiot," Lillian agreed, "but you shouldn't give him up so easily. I know you like him, and why not? He's an amazing man and he is good in bed, which is a bonus."

"If he doesn't want me, why should I want him?" Jane asked stubbornly.

"Because he's a stubborn fool," Lillian said. "And he needs to be made to see reason."

Jane sighed. It wasn't that she didn't want to make Sidney see reason, but she was sad that Lillian pleaded his case so much. Was that because she didn't want to be with Jane and wanted to let her down gently?

She took a deep breath and took a decision. "Lillian, I don't know if I want to be with Sidney," she said.

Lillian's hand, high on her thigh now, almost touching her rapidly soaking panties, distracted her, but she ignored the effect it was having on her.

"I love you, Lillian," she pressed on. "And I want to spend my life with you."

She held her breath at these last words. Lillian didn't speak for a moment, but Jane could see emotions battle on her face.

"I love you too," Lillian whispered. "But I really don't know if we can be together."

Jane's heart soared at Lillian's declaration of love and she leaned over and kissed her. "Don't say we can't be together. Why not? If we both love each other, what can possibly stand in our way?"

"My profession," Lillian said, her eyes on the ground. "I have a contract and I need to travel the country, and possibly the world, singing in different clubs. I can't ask you to come with me for that."

"Are you ashamed of our relationship?" Jane felt a slight wobble in her heart.

"No!" Lillian's head shot up, her eyes ablaze. "There is nothing shameful about our love. I just can't ask of you to travel with me, or to stay home and wait for me."

Jane cupped her face gently. "Oh Lillian, I would wait until the end of eternity for you," she whispered. "I've never met someone who made me this happy – and this satisfied."

"Are you sure about this?" Lillian asked.

"I've never been more certain in my entire life. I fell in love with you the first time I met you, and my love for you has only grown. I would move heaven and earth to be with you."

Lillian leaned over and kissed her. "I love you too. I just thought you'd choose Sidney over me."

Jane's face darkened. "I meant what I said before, if

Sidney doesn't want me, then I'm not going to fight for him."

"Oh, Jane," Lillian sighed. "You are so innocent and naïve. Of course he wants you, he's just too proud to admit it."

"Doesn't matter," Jane said. "I chose you, didn't I?"

Lillian smiled. "That's true. But our love is not conventional. It won't be as easy to explain to people as marrying Sidney would."

"I love you," Jane said stubbornly. "And I won't make any excuses for it."

"But you love Sidney too," Lillian said.

Jane's heart sank. "I do," she confessed. "But I want to be with you."

"And I want to be with you."

"Then let's not speak of Sidney again," Jane said as her mouth found Lillian's again.

CHAPTER 26

Jane lived on cloud nine for the next few days. Sidney remained in New York and she didn't hear from him, but she wasn't concerned. He would tell her in due course what she needed to know. In the meantime, she wanted to savour every minute with Lillian. They swam together, walked along the river for hours and spent every night together. Rachel had given up trying to spend time with them. She had hugged Jane and told her how happy she was for her.

On the fourth day, Jane was getting anxious. She still had not heard anything from Sidney and the cold hand of fear gripped her heart. What if there were complications? What if Uncle Henry had squandered away all her money and she was penniless?

"Don't worry so much," Lillian soothed when Jane had returned to the house after another fruitless walk down the drive to see if Sidney was returning yet. "He'll be here soon and I'm sure he'll have good news."

"What if he doesn't?" Jane asked. "What if I don't have any money? What will I do?"

"You'll still have me," Lillian said. "And I'm not exactly poor myself."

Jane kissed her. "You're so wonderful, but I don't have any skills."

"You'll be fine, didn't Sidney say that the investments weren't touched?"

Jane sighed. She wasn't sure anymore what Sidney had said. It all seemed too good to be true. She had woken this morning thinking it had all been a dream. The longer Sidney stayed away, the less she dared hope everything was going to turn out all right.

"I'm scared," she said.

Lillian hugged her. "At the very least you have your home," she said. "Stop worrying and let's do something fun."

Jane attempted a smile. "Like what?"

Lillian grinned. "I can think of a few things…"

She pulled Jane closer and kissed her. Jane closed her eyes and kissed Lillian back. She needed to escape her fears for a while, and this could help make her feel better.

Lillian slid her hands underneath Jane's skirt and cupped her ass. Jane could feel the familiar throb in her lower belly and she relaxed into Lillian's embrace. It felt so good to be touched like this.

She broke the kiss and gasped as Lillian slipped one hand inside her panties, her fingers sliding through her folds. Right at that moment, her ears picked up the sound of a car approaching and she grabbed Lillian's hand to stop her.

Lillian's eyes snapped open. "What's wrong?"

"Did you hear that?" Jane asked.

Lillian cocked her head. "The car?"

"Yes, I think that might be Sidney." Jane pulled herself out of Lillian's embrace and hurried to the window in time to see Sidney get out of the car. "It's him, let's go downstairs."

Lillian groaned. "What bad timing."

Jane grabbed her hand and pulled her towards the door. "If he has good news we can celebrate properly," she said. "Come on!"

They ran down the stairs and met Sidney in the entrance hall. He looked sombre and tired. Jane's breath caught and fear gripped her heart.

"Sidney," she called out, as if he hadn't heard them running down the stairs. "What news?"

Sidney smiled when he turned towards her. "Good news, Matthew and I have been able to fix everything for you."

"Oh, that is wonderful!" Jane cried and threw herself into his arms. He caught her and pulled her close. She reached on tiptoes and kissed him without thinking. His reticence from before was gone, and he returned her kisses passionately.

"Let's go out into the garden," Lillian said behind them. "Rachel will want to hear the news too. Did Matthew come back with you?"

Jane pulled herself away from Sidney, suddenly feeling guilty at her display of affection. She had pledged herself to Lillian; it was inappropriate to kiss Sidney.

"I'm sorry," she said. "I forgot myself. You're right, we should go and sit down. And you may want something refreshing, Sidney," she added.

"Matthew stayed in the city with Richard. He sends his regards, though."

He put his arm around Jane and then reached out for Lillian. She came to his other side and together they walked out into the garden.

Rachel was brought up to speed as soon as Sidney had quenched his thirst. Jane held Lillian's hand while Sidney explained that Uncle Henry had indeed only been able to inhabit the house. All the money was still untouched, and what was more: the intervening years had increased her investments so that she was a very wealthy woman now. Jane could not believe her ears when he told her the magnitude of her wealth; she would never have to worry about money again. She felt almost delirious with relief. Everything was going to be all right.

The only thing that cast a shadow on her happiness was Sidney himself. Not because he treated her badly; quite the opposite. When he had departed, Jane had been convinced that he didn't want anything to do with her anymore. Lillian's words about Sidney not wanting to marry a rich woman had struck a chord with her and she had believed him to be an unreasonable man. But the Sidney who had returned from New York was quite different. He was happy, exuberant almost, and most attentive to her. He was back to his old self: sweet, kind, and flirty. She should have been happy about that, but instead it made her feel worse.

Had Sidney still been reticent towards her, she would have felt vindicated at her decision to choose Lillian. She had thought he was no longer interested in her, and that had made her decision so much easier. Not that she considered severing ties with Lillian. She loved Lillian. More than she had ever loved anyone in her life. And she could not imagine life without her.

On the other hand, she loved Sidney as well. He was her childhood crush and he was just as attractive to her as an adult as he had been when she had been a young woman. She wanted to be with him, but she didn't want to give up Lillian. Her heart was a tangled mess of confused emotions, which made it very hard for her to enjoy the good news of her newfound wealth. While the others were toasting her with glasses of champagne, she smiled wanly and tried to make sense of her feelings.

What was she supposed to do? Society would approve of her breaking her relationship with Lillian and choosing Sidney instead. Her heart, however, had different desires. She did not want to choose. Not because the choice was too difficult – impossible even – but because she wanted to be with both Lillian and Sidney. Why should she have to choose? She loved them both and they liked each other. They had had amazing sex together, so they were compatible in that area as well. Why did she have to choose?

She sighed and drained her glass of champagne. She set the empty glass back on the table and got up. Four heads swivelled towards her.

"I'm going for a walk," she said. "It's all a bit overwhelming."

Lillian and Sidney shared a glance, but Jane didn't want to try to interpret it. She needed to be alone for a while, clear her head. She couldn't think with all of them present.

The river was the most obvious place to go and Jane walked until she rounded a bend and could not see the house anymore. Then she sat down on a fallen log, her head in her hands. What was she supposed to do? She was rich, she had a wonderful girlfriend she loved and a home of her own. Her whole life had suddenly improved a hundredfold and yet she wasn't happy. She greedily also wanted to have Sidney. But things didn't work that way.

She kicked off her shoes and walked towards the edge of the water. She dipped her feet into the river and sighed at the coolness. Her thoughts were going round and round in circles, but she never got any further than the certain knowledge that she loved Sidney as much as she loved Lillian. It wasn't fair that she had to choose.

A movement beside her made her look up. Sidney walked towards her, a smile on his face.

"I know you wanted to clear your head, but I wanted to make sure you're all right," he said. "You seemed a bit withdrawn earlier."

Jane walked back to the log and sat down again. Sidney sat down next to her.

"I'm fine," she said. "I've just found out I'm rich, what more could I want?"

Sidney laughed a short laugh. "I must apologise for my behaviour before I departed for the city."

Jane waved his apology away. "It doesn't matter."

He took her hand in his. "But it does matter. I don't want you to think that I don't care about you. I do care about you. I just needed to get my head wrapped around the idea that I was in love with a very wealthy woman."

Jane's heart skipped a beat. "In love?" she repeated.

Sidney gently cupped her chin and lifted her head. She looked into his dark eyes and saw only love.

"I love you, Jane," he said.

"I love you too," she said.

"Then why are you looking so unhappy?"

Jane looked away from him. "Because I also love Lillian."

Sidney sighed. "I know."

She looked at him. "You know?"

"I'm not blind," he said. "I can see you two have a special relationship."

"I want to be with you," Jane said. "But I also want to be with Lillian. I can't choose between you two."

Lillian's voice suddenly sounded behind them. "Don't choose then."

Jane looked up. Lillian approached them and sat down on her other side on the log. She took her hand.

"If you love both of us, you can have both of us. Right?" she added to Sidney.

Jane looked around to Sidney.

He nodded slowly. "Of course she can."

Hope began to dawn in Jane's chest. "Do you mean…" she started, almost afraid to speak the idea aloud.

"We can all be together," Lillian said. "Sidney and I like each other and we both love you. Why should we force you to choose?"

"But…" Jane said. But society will never accept this, she wanted to say. We can never get married, all three of us.

182

Lillian kissed her. "You and Sidney can get married and you and I can have an affair." She winked. "We can all live together and no one needs to know the truth. No one we don't want to tell the truth, at least."

"And we already know the sex is amazing," Sidney added with a chuckle.

Hope bloomed in Jane's heart. "This could work, couldn't it?" she said.

"Of course," Lillian said.

Jane grabbed her hand and pressed it to her lips. Tears sprang to her eyes. "Are you serious about this?"

Lillian and Sidney both put their arms around Jane. "Absolutely," Sidney said.

"Wouldn't want it any other way," Lillian agreed.

"Then yes," Jane said, her heart bursting with joy. "Yes, I choose you both. I love you and I want to spend my life with both of you."

CHAPTER 27

They had taken Rachel into their confidence along with Matthew and Richard who had driven down from the city the next day. It was only fair that they knew the truth as well, as Rachel had facilitated their meeting – and falling in love. Matthew and Richard had offered their congratulations. It wasn't lost on Jane the situation might be difficult for Matthew and Richard, who would never be able to get married, or even live together as lovers.

Rachel had been ecstatic and had suggested Jane and Sidney got married right away. Jane was in favour, but Sidney wanted to give his parents more notice. Jane didn't care whether Uncle Henry and Aunt Lydia approved or not. She was no longer dependent on them.

It would take another few days for all the paperwork to come together. Sidney was planning to take her to New York when everything was ready. Jane's victory over Uncle Henry felt bittersweet. She was happy to have her home back, and to know she could live without the shadow of him hanging over her, but at the same time she couldn't be too harsh on him. Or, at least not on Aunt Lydia. They had taken her in when she had lost her parents and while they had repressed her, they had provided a roof over her head and food on the table.

"You're too soft," Lillian complained that night in bed when Jane confided in her.

Jane trailed kisses down her neck towards her breast. "No, I'm not," she said softly. "I just don't see the point in being mean to them. Once they're back in New York I don't have to deal with them. Uncle Henry knows he's lost and I don't need to remind him of my victory."

Sidney ran his hand over Jane's ass, stopping short from her cunt. "You should at least tell them you're getting married."

Jane spread her legs to allow him access. "I don't see why. I'm of age, I can decide whom I marry. I don't need them to ruin the day."

"Oh, but they won't ruin the day," Lillian said, caressing the back of Jane's head and guiding her to her erect nipple. "We can tell them exactly what's going on and the look on Henry's face alone would be priceless."

Jane took Lillian's nipple in her mouth and bit it gently. Lillian moaned softly.

"No," she said. "Uncle Henry will try to find a way to ruin everything, I just want him out of my life."

Sidney slid his hand between Jane's thighs, his fingers briefly touching her clit. Jane's breath hitched. Lillian guided Jane lower, towards her own cunt and she obliged. She parted Lillian's puffy outer lips and sought her centre with her tongue. Lillian moaned as Jane's tongue made contact with her clit. Without preamble, Jane pushed two fingers inside her and curled them up, seeking out Lillian's special spot.

Sidney spread Jane's legs wider and slid his cock between her folds, coating it in her juices. Jane found it hard to concentrate on Lillian when her own cunt was throbbing to be filled. Sidney teased her, pressing the tip of his cock inside her before withdrawing it again. Jane tried to be patient and focus on Lillian, but her whole body craved to be filled. She pushed her hips back in an attempt to take in more of Sidney.

A stinging slap landed on her ass and she gasped at the impact.

"Stay still, slut," Sidney growled near her ear. He reached around her and pinched her nipple hard.

She gasped with delight. Sidney and Lillian always knew exactly what she needed, and right now she needed them to shut up and be rough with her. She didn't want to think, only feel. It was good to be with both Lillian and Sidney and the thought that this didn't need to end when summer was over filled Jane with happiness.

Eager for another slap, she wriggled her hips again and was rewarded immediately.

"Do I need to spank you?" Sidney asked harshly.

Jane looked over her shoulder at him. "If you think I deserve it," she said, grinning.

Sidney drew himself up. "I do think you deserve it," he said.

"Get on with it," Lillian said. "Make her lick me while you do it; there's no reason she should neglect her duties to me."

Jane looked around at her and smiled. "I'll make sure to focus on you," she said meekly.

"Then get to it," Lillian commanded. "I've been patient enough with you."

Jane obeyed and resumed her position between Lillian's legs. She tried to ignore Sidney behind her, who seemed to derive pleasure from letting her wait. Her thighs were coated with her juices of anticipation and desire.

Lillian grabbed her head and kept it in place. Jane teased Lillian's clit until it was erect and peeking from under its hood. She swirled her tongue around the little bud while pressing her fingers deep inside Lillian's wet cunt. She loved the hot, tight feeling around her fingers, the juices seeping out of Lillian and covering her hand and face. She inhaled Lillian's smell, so different from her own, and marvelled, not for the first time, how amazing it was to bring another woman to her climax.

Her attention was so focused on Lillian that she wasn't prepared for the hard slap from Sidney. She moaned when it landed, lower than the first two slaps. His fingers brushed her exposed sex and she moaned again. He carefully meted out another slap on her other ass cheek, his fingers again brushing her cunt. Two more slaps followed in rapid succession and Jane tried to keep still as his hand moved closer and closer to her cunt.

"Focus," Lillian ordered her. "You'll not be allowed to have an orgasm until you've made me come."

Jane whimpered and redoubled her efforts on Lillian's cunt. She sucked and licked and rubbed until she could feel Lillian's cunt tighten around her fingers. Her whole being was concentrated on the spanking on her ass and cunt, and the effort to bring Lillian to an orgasm.

Lillian grabbed her head and held her tight against her cunt, pressing herself up against Jane's mouth. She moaned and writhed on the bed while Jane tried her hardest not to allow her own climax to take her over. Sidney's spanks eased off and he moved his hand down so it fully covered her cunt. His fingers touched her clit on each slap and Jane's body was taut with the effort not to come. Her own fingers and tongue worked frantically on Lillian's cunt and at last, Lillian cried out and pushed Jane's head away. She convulsed around Jane's fingers, moaning and crying at once.

"Good girl," Sidney whispered, immediately ceasing his spanking. "Now for your reward."

Jane could barely hold herself up on her elbows as Sidney replaced his hands with his cock. He pushed inside her and she cried out with relief. Lillian sat up and reached for Jane's cunt. Her fingers found Jane's clit and she thrummed it expertly while Sidney pounded into her.

The frustrating wait combined with the sensation of Sidney's spanking had driven Jane to the brink of orgasm and she moaned and cried as wave after wave of pleasure crashed over her. Her cunt contracted around Sidney's cock as the first of her orgasms took her. Sidney did not slow down, nor did Lillian and soon the tension rose in Jane again, carrying her towards the crest. This time Sidney came as well, releasing his seed inside her with a groan.

Reduced to a blubbering mess, Jane fell down on the bed. Sidney lay down next to her and cradled her while Lillian moved to position herself between Jane's legs.

"My reward," she whispered as she spread Jane wide.

Jane sighed with delight as Lillian's tongue soothed her sore, swollen cunt, licking all traces of Sidney's seed out of her.

"Not too sore?" Sidney asked.

Jane nodded sleepily. "It was perfect. I can't wait to do this with you two every night."

Lillian chuckled and moved to lie on Jane's other side. "Maybe not every night," she said. "We don't want to hurt you too badly."

Jane rolled over and faced Lillian. "It doesn't have to be this rough every night," she said. "But spending every night with you and Sidney will be heaven, whether there's sex involved or not."

Lillian kissed her. "I think we can manage sex every night," she whispered.

"Between the two of us we'll make sure to keep you satisfied," Sidney said. "You did really well tonight."

Warmth suffused Jane as she lay cradled in the arms of the two people she loved most. Her future, so bleak at the beginning of the summer, looked full of love, pleasure and joy.

ABOUT THE AUTHOR

Isabelle Lauren is a writer and blogger. When she's not writing, she loves reading, crocheting or walking her pug.

Her blog can be found at https://isabellelauren.com.

Printed in Poland
by Amazon Fulfillment
Poland Sp. z o.o., Wrocław

51366240R00115